A MURDER MOST MACABRE

Jeremy Lavelle, leader of the esoteric Egyptian Society the Order of the True Sphinx, has illegally purchased an ancient Egyptian mummy. Watched by his enthralled followers, he opens the coffin and begins to unwrap the body ... The head is that of an ancient scribe, his shrivelled and desiccated face staring eyelessly up from his coffin — yet from the neck down, wrapped up in layers of bandages, are not the mummified remains which they had expected. Instead, they stare in horror at the decapitated corpse of a recently killed man!

EDMUND GLASBY

A MURDER MOST MACABRE

Complete and Unabridged

LINFORD
Leicester

First published in Great Britain

First Linford Edition
published 2015

A catalogue record for this book is available
from the British Library.

ISBN 978–1–4448–2556–5

Published by
F. A. Thorpe (Publishing)
Anstey, Leicestershire

Set by Words & Graphics Ltd.
Anstey, Leicestershire
Printed and bound in Great Britain by
T. J. International Ltd., Padstow, Cornwall

This book is printed on acid-free paper

1

Jeremy Lavelle was well known in certain circles — strange circles. A University of Oxford dropout, he had turned his pseudo-academic talents to the study and promotion of the obscure subject of Egyptomania; not that he would refer to it in such a derogatory manner. To him, *his* was the authentic study of Ancient Egypt, as opposed to that which was undertaken by the official experts in the field. To this end, he had established a society known as the Order of the True Sphinx, organising talks and holding lectures on some of the more fanciful topics surrounding Ancient Egypt: its history, culture, religion and archaeology. Drawing on his substantial knowledge, he would embellish the accepted and the conventional with the weird and the esoteric, filling the minds of those easily misguided stalwarts who attended his meetings with all manner of New Age nonsense. This ranged from theorising that the pyramids had been built with alien intervention through to the idea that the ancient Egyptians were derived from Atlantean stock.

It was arguable whether he was merely a charlatan peddling his unorthodox concepts to the like-minded and the gullible, or someone who genuinely believed in what he preached; for although initially he had been in it only for the money and the sense of power that came with 'enlightening' others, over time he himself had come to accept many of these unsubstantiated notions. Indeed, his pursuits into the more fringe aspects of Egyptology had now become an obsession, to the extent that tonight — in addition to celebrating his fiftieth birthday and the fiftieth anniversary of a rather famous archaeological discovery — he had something very special planned.

★　★　★

Resplendent in his full ancient Egyptian pharaonic regalia: a fabulous embroidered robe, a jewelled collar and an ornate nemes headdress complete with a gilt uraeus, the striking cobra which symbolised kingship, Lavelle strode solemnly down the wide staircase.

His twenty or so guests who were standing below turned and gazed, awestruck. Some raised their glasses and began to cheer. Others, who had made the effort and had dressed in similar, though not as grand, clothing, knelt or bowed, gesticulating subserviently with hand flourishes. One individual even went as far as to prostrate himself on the tiled floor.

Smugly, Lavelle continued down the stairs. He gestured with his hand for the man on the floor to get up. 'Arise, Child of the Nile!' he said.

The man got to his feet.

Lavelle beamed inwardly. He had remained on the second step so that he could tower slightly over those before him. Looking down on the gathered men and women, he could not help but feel superior to them. It really was as though he were a god-king lording it over his subjects; or rather a cult leader being worshipped by his disciples. For a moment, he basked in the admiration. Then, raising his arms, both in order to get their attention and to cast a surreptitious glance at his wristwatch, he said: 'The festivities will commence shortly. May I ask you all to make your way into the dining room where the banquet awaits. Please, follow me.' Leading the way, he set off down the hall, his guests close behind.

The dining-room door was sealed with a red-and-gold banner covered with ancient Egyptian hieroglyphs. A huge gilt ankh — the symbol of life — had been nailed to the wood.

Lavelle paused. Raising a hand, the fingers of which were adorned with gold and lapis lazuli scarab rings, he brought everyone to a halt. Following the alphabetic symbols from right to left, he began reading out words that had no relation whatsoever to what was written there. 'Praise to thee, Osiris, Giver of Life and God of the Underworld! For to him who enters here a wondrous bounty awaits!' Dramatically, he then tore down

4

the seal, hastily scrunching it up and putting it in a pocket of his robe just in case there was anyone present who *could* translate ancient Egyptian hieroglyphics. 'With the blessing of Osiris, we may enter.' He reached out and pushed the door wide.

The dining room was dominated by a long table which had been extravagantly set out with all manner of exotic foodstuffs, buffet-style, although this was unlike any self-service feast anyone present had ever attended before. It was abundantly clear that Lavelle had gone to great expense in order to throw his lavish party. In addition to the unusual gourmet dishes which included gazelle cutlets, poached quail, slivers of roasted croco-dile, spiced heron stuffed with olives, and half a dozen other mouth-watering exotic meats, there was a wide range of equally bizarre vegetable and salad accompani-ments, each one a delicacy in its own right.

The drinks, too, were varied. As well as the normal spirits and liquors there was a somewhat sludgy barley beer which had supposedly been fermented and brewed in accordance with ancient Egyptian practice. Whilst nourishing, it had a low alcohol content and one sip of its bitterness was usually enough to dissuade those with a discerning palate from having any more.

The diners began to help themselves to the bountiful fare. Some were reluctant to try the stranger dishes on offer whilst others, those perhaps of a more adventurous disposition, willingly experimented, sampling all that was available, knowing, perhaps, that they would never get this opportunity again. To indulge in some of the truly outlandish food on offer was surely a once-in-a-lifetime experience.

Those present were frequent attendees of Lavelle's talks and consequently many of them knew each other, and had done so for many years. They were all people of a similar background and education, but more importantly they, like their host, were all wealthy individuals — professionals who had both the time and the means to support such an eccentric cause. All believed fervently, almost to the point of indoctrination, in Lavelle's teachings, enraptured by the idea that the ancient Egyptians had been in possession of powers and secrets far in advance of what they were given credit for.

Thirty minutes or so into the feast, Lavelle, who was seated at the head of the table in a large wooden throne which was surmounted by the Aten — the sun-disc which had been venerated by the heretical pharaoh Akhenaten — rose to his feet. He took off his elaborate headdress and put it down on the table. 'A most cumbersome thing to have to wear,' he commented. 'Anyway, I trust everyone is enjoying themselves, and may I personally thank you all for coming to my little soirée. I truly appreciate it. May I also take this opportunity to thank you for your ongoing support and patronage. Without you the Order would be unable to survive.' He cleared his throat. 'As you are all no doubt aware, today I celebrate my half-century.'

There were several cries of, 'Many happy returns!' Someone started up with a rendition of 'Happy Birthday'.

Lavelle looked slightly embarrassed throughout. When the song had finished, he raised a hand to get his guests' attention. 'Today, November twenty-sixth, also marks the fiftieth anniversary of the discovery, or rather the opening, of the tomb of Tutankhamen by Howard Carter and Lord Carnarvon in the Valley of the Kings in 1922. This sensational event — and let's not forget the curse which followed — led to a resurgence throughout England, and indeed the world at large, of all things pertaining to ancient Egypt.

'However, the fascination with this glorious civilisation can be traced back much further into antiquity. From Napoleonic times and the discovery of the Rosetta Stone through into the occult and Masonic symbolism of the early eighteenth century, there has been widespread usage, and indeed emulation, of its art, architecture and religion. Ask yourself: Why it is that the pyramid and the wadjet — the all-seeing eye of Horus — feature so predominantly on the American dollar bill? Just why did Hitler authorise a top-secret mission to infiltrate and steal certain arte-facts from the Ashmolean Museum, in particular the Scorpion Macehead which it is well known possesses unprecedented mystical energy? Several of his agents were also plotting the dismantling of Cleopatra's Needle in order to transfer it to Berlin.'

These latter two statements were pure bunkum which he had read in one of the more outrageous publications which he subscribed to, but nevertheless they all served to enhance his reputation and sense of self-importance. He knew and relished the fact that he had a certain charismatic appeal which was undoubt-edly strengthened by playing up his erudite and esoteric personality.

'As you know, I myself am in possession of some of the lesser-known mystical rites and funerary incantations — I suppose one would call them spells, which were closely guarded by the high priests of Thoth. And it is only because of this that I am able to show you something very special indeed. Something which I am sure none of you will have ever seen before. I myself have seen this performed

9

but once, and that was long ago in a dusty hovel on the outskirts of Cairo.'

The solemnity with which Lavelle made this last announcement prompted many to sit up. There were several bewildered faces. Just what was it they were about to witness? Some considered their host to be something of a sorcerer; after all, he had just admitted as much. Perhaps he was going to astound them with a demonstration of practical ancient Egyptian magic of the kind to be found within the sacred *Pyramid Texts* or that which had been utilised to varying degrees of success by the notorious occultist Aleister Crowley.

'Now then, if everyone has finished, I would ask you to please follow me.' With a swish of his cloak, Lavelle left the table and headed for the door, stepping out into the hall. He then took a left turn, heading towards the back of the house, striding dramatically.

There was some interested muttering amongst his guests. Chairs were pushed back as they got to their feet and followed, eager to find out what new thrill awaited them. There was something almost sinister in the way in which they processed down the shadowy corridor, its walls decorated with countless pieces of ancient Egyptian Old, Middle and New Kingdom art — none of which was authentic, but still looked the part.

Lavelle stopped outside his study. Like the door to the dining room, this one also had a seal covering it. Disregarding the light switch which would have bathed the corridor in unwanted illumination, he reached for a torch which he had put previously on a nearby chair, turned it on and directed the beam of light onto the miniscule pictorial script. Once more he began his fraudulent deciphering: 'Beware he who enters here. This is the tomb of Aj-Merak, Scribe of Ptah, son of Kheph-tat. It is guarded by Anubis, Lord of the Necropolis and Protector of the Dead. A thousand curses on he who would defile this place without first offering the proper prayers.'

Somewhat irreverently, given the situation, someone at the back of the corridor broke out into a sneezing fit, spoiling for a time the intended ambience. And whilst many had now come to accept that all of this was just a little theatrical role-playing, it was certainly different as well as entertaining; far better than spending the evening playing charades or 'what's my line'. Whether it would culminate in an alcohol-induced, wife-swapping orgiastic revel, as some privately hoped, remained to be seen. However, given the way things were going . . .

Uttering a stream of strangely syllabic words, Lavelle went down on one knee. A minute later he got to his feet and, palms outstretched, pushed the door forward an inch. Taking his torch, he shone the light inside. 'I can see . . . *wonderful things*,' he said, trying his best to re-enact the initial moments of Carter's famous discovery. Those nearest to him eagerly edged forward, wanting to participate in the mystery of it all.

Pushing the door wider, Lavelle stepped inside his study. From the light of his torch it could be seen that he had gone to great lengths in transforming the room into a mock-up of an ancient Egyptian

Middle Kingdom tomb.

The wooden floorboards had been covered with sand, amidst which numerous replicas of pharaonic grave goods lay. There were half a dozen large pottery urns, an overturned chariot, two senet boards, many animal-headed statues of wood and alabaster, and a whole array of other miscellaneous treasures. The walls and windows were covered with long cloth drapes upon which had been painted a diverse range of ancient Egyptian tomb scenes. The overall effect was highly impressive and, certainly at first glance, extremely realistic.

'Please step carefully,' Lavelle warned, making his way further into the 'tomb'.

There were amazed looks and approving comments as everyone else shuffled cautiously inside. The area was large enough for all to get into, even with the replica funerary items which lay scattered haphazardly around. For many, this truly was a unique experience — and whilst undoubtedly surreal, it was in all likelihood the closest they would ever come to being in a genuine ancient

Egyptian tomb. There was even a faint but detectable odour in the room — a musty, age-old smell that, whilst not particularly pleasant, added to the overall effect. Whatever else could be said about this transformed study, it was certainly not tacky. A lot of time, money and expertise had gone into it.

Purposefully shading the torch with his hand, Lavelle moved to the back of the room. 'Imagine you are now deep under the Saqqaran Necropolis, gathered in the Memphite burial chamber of Aj-Merak. Whilst admittedly rare, during the nineteenth century it was recorded that the aristocrats of the day sometimes threw what were known as mummy unwrapping parties. Tonight, on this prestigious occasion, it is my intention to do the same.'

A hushed, excited mutter came from the darkness. Everyone had been expecting something fairly spectacular, but this went beyond their wildest dreams. There were a few there besides Lavelle who knew that the unscientific unwrapping of mummies had been going on for a lot longer than a hundred or so years. There had once been, and to some extent still was, a clandestine, lucrative and highly illegal trade in ancient cadavers, both for the morbidly curious and the medical profession. Mummia — which referred to both the bitumen-based substance used in the embalming process and the powdery residue product from the grinding-up process — remained highly sought after by alternative doctors, alchemists and occultists, for it was believed to possess regenerative and magical properties. Indeed, such had been the demand for it that mummies had been ground up on an almost industrial scale in so-called mummy-mills. As genuine mummified corpses became harder to procure, those operating in this nefarious trade had improvised by unearthing the recently buried and using them as substitutes, most buyers being none the wiser.

Raising the torch so that the beam of light fell full on the long oblong box that rested on the table before him, Lavelle said: 'Behold! The sarcophagus of Aj-Merak. Inside rest the sacredly embalmed remains of a Middle Kingdom scribe of the Twelfth

Dynasty. For over three and a half thousand years his body has been encased within. Tonight, we shall gaze upon him.'

Positioning himself on the side opposite the onlookers, he reached over and picked up a box of matches. He lit two tall candles which stood in ornate silver candlesticks, producing a slightly repellent and oleaginous whiff. Now that the candles threw an atmospheric glow over the room, he switched off his torch, its luminosity surplus to requirements. Shadows danced within the sepulchral chamber.

Forming a tightly-packed semicircle around the crate-like container, Lavelle's guests stood in awe and wonder, eagerly anticipating that which was to come. The fact that they were about to participate in something which would be considered absolutely reprehensible by the serious Egyptological community was of no concern to them whatsoever.

The wooden sarcophagus itself was fairly unremarkable in appearance, being little more than a rough, vaguely man-sized casket, the sides of which featured faint traces of painted designs and the odd

16

band of ancient Egyptian hieroglyphics. Certainly it was far removed from the fabulous golden coffin in which Tutankhamen had been interred but, nevertheless, it held its own aura of mystique.

'No doubt some of you are wondering just how I managed to acquire such a treasure.' Lavelle looked admiringly down at the discoloured lid, as eager and as curious to prise it open as those before him. 'Well, believe me, it wasn't easy. I've been searching for something like this for many years and, thanks to our outdated and imbecilic laws which prohibit trade in such antiquities, I was forced to both make use of my extensive circle of contacts and deal with some very shady individuals. Suffice to say, obtaining it was neither cheap nor easy. Now, no doubt some of you may be questioning its authenticity. Well, let me assure you that this *is* the real thing. One only has to examine the *Coffin Texts* inscribed upon the surfaces, or feel the ancient cedar which would have been imported from the coast of distant Lebanon, to ascertain that.'

Lovingly, he did just that, stroking his

hand over the lid. He looked up, half-expecting someone to ask a question, but for the time being they were all captivated by his actions.

A phone somewhere in another room began to ring, its incongruous sound temporarily infringing on the silence and upsetting the moment.

Lavelle gave a disgruntled nod of his head and waited until it had quietened down again. Reaching over to one side, he drew back a sheet of cloth which covered a wooden tray upon which rested a collection of gleaming surgical implements; scalpels, knives, scissors, a wicked-looking bone saw, and even a mallet and chisel. 'Now, I don't profess to having any specific anatomical training, but one of the things which I will be endeavouring to discover is whether or not this mummy has had its internal organs removed as was customary during the embalming process. No doubt you are all aware that it was the norm for the stomach, lungs, intestines and liver to be stored within canopic jars, but occasionally mummies have been found with their organs in situ.

I trust no one here is of a squeamish disposition. If you are, then may I suggest that you leave the room when I get to that stage. But firstly, we must open it up.'

Not a word was spoken as the spectators took several steps forward.

Wedging the chisel under the lid, Lavelle gave the handle several taps with the mallet, forcing the wooden covering up. He had only raised it a couple of inches, but the smell which emanated from within was eye-wateringly putrid. It was something he had not prepared himself for and, gagging slightly, he stepped back.

The stench had now reached his guests. As one, they too recoiled, noses wrinkling in disgust.

Lavelle recovered quickly. 'Whilst most unfortunate, I suppose the smell is to be expected. Now that the hermetic seal is breached, the age-old perfumes and resins which would have been used by the Middle Kingdom morticians have no doubt reacted, creating this rather unpleasant scent.' With a few more taps on the chisel, he succeeded in levering one edge of the lid up. Moving further down the coffin, he inserted the chisel and repeated the process.

The candle flames guttered.

With a final strike on the chisel, the lid flew up.

The reek that blasted out from the now fully opened funerary container was horrendous. It was as though a long-closed manhole cover had been lifted.

Fighting back the revulsion, Lavelle looked down at the linen-swathed shape, the bandages filthy and ragged. The arms were crossed over the chest in the typical burial position and there was a band of brown-red discolouring around the neck and some around the abdomen, no doubt due to where the body had been operated on in antiquity. Wafting the foul air aside, he then took hold of the rigid arms. These he moved so that they hung over the edge of the coffin. He picked up a large pair of scissors. Nausea, excitement and apprehension raged through his body, causing his stomach muscles to tighten. He felt light-headed, giddy almost. He knew that the sensation he was now feeling had to be similar to that which Carter had experienced fifty years ago — the stepping into the unknown; the discovery of that which had been long-buried. For a moment, he was uncertain as to where to start.

'It's amazing!' voiced Charles Braithwaite, an elderly bespectacled man who wrote horror stories for a living. 'Truly amazing!'

'To think that this predates the birth of Christ by fifteen hundred years or more and that we're the first to see it,' remarked a glamorous raven-haired woman named Sylvia Black. Dressed as she was in a long golden lamé gown, she bore more than a passing resemblance to Elizabeth Taylor in her portrayal of the Queen of the Nile from the 1963 film *Cleopatra*. 'Why, Jeremy, it's . . . unbelievable!' she exclaimed.

'Yes, it certainly is. It's a pity about the smell though.' With an effort, Lavelle forced himself to be calm, to still his trembling arms and fingers. In order not to execute this procedure in a crude and disrespectful manner, he would need to be focused. The last thing he wanted was for this to become just a ghoulish dissection; a slapdash autopsy. No, this had to be done with the element of reverence

21

and professionalism it deserved. Carefully, delicately, he began to cut down from a position a couple of inches below the jaw-line with the intention of exposing what would undoubtedly be the leather-hardened, partly desiccated skin beneath. It proved to be quite tough going. The linen had been wound tightly, and in places it was like cutting through a thick carpet.

'Do you think the mummy will be naked, or will it be clothed in some kind of garment?' asked Don Hardwick. An American financier who had made millions in both New York and London, he was by far the richest man there. Lavelle aside, he was also the most fanatic member of the Order, having made considerable donations to it.

'And what level of preservation do you think we can expect?' inquired Sylvia.

'I'm not sure what state we'll find it in . . . but we'll discover that soon enough,' answered Lavelle, peeling back a swathe of grimy bandage. 'If we're lucky there may even be some amulets incorporated within the wrappings — scarabs and periapts which would protect the dead on the journey to the afterlife.'

'What are you going to do with it afterwards?' queried Braithwaite. He was probably hoping that Lavelle would entertain the idea of selling it to him. As a horror writer, it would be more than welcome in his house and would be undoubtedly less argumentative than his wife.

Lavelle looked up. 'I don't know. I haven't thought that far ahead. I might see about taking a part of it, a hand or a foot for example, and making some of my own mummia extract. If I do, I'll be sure to provide you all with a small sample. The beneficial properties are rumoured to be — ' He stopped upon hearing a dull-sounding metallic clink caused by the scissors striking something. 'It would appear that there may well be — ' He stopped a second time. Surely to God that was not a belt buckle? This was . . . *unusual*, to say the least. Swallowing a lump in his throat, he tore away at the bindings, exposing a blood-stained che-quered shirt and a pair of denim jeans.

2

Lavelle, Hardwick, Braithwaite and two others — Peter Hoffman, a retired doctor and Larry Williams, a university lecturer who taught philosophy — were seated around the now-cleared dining room table. An hour and a half had passed since the gruesome find — made worse by the discovery that the head was, in all likelihood, that of Aj-Merak, his shrivelled and desiccated rotted brown face staring eyelessly up from what was still considered to be an authentic Middle Kingdom coffin. It was macabre. Utterly ghoulish.

Upon the immediate and shocking realisation that the being from the neck down, wrapped up in the layers of bandages, was not the mummified remains which he had hoped for, Lavelle had turned instantly to Hoffman, aware of his medical background.

Stunned and horrified, the two of them had then proceeded to extricate the bloody, decapitated corpse. It had proved to be grisly work, for the body had undergone a fair amount of decomposition; and whilst Lavelle had prepared himself for dissecting a three-and-a-half-thousand-year-old mummy, to be suddenly faced with a much more recent corpse had been hard going.

The badly decomposed body, once fully exposed, was that of a slightly built male of indeterminate age. From a cursory examination, Hoffman believed that in addition to having been beheaded, he had been stabbed several times in the stomach. Apart from his bloodstained shirt, denim jeans and underpants, there were no other items of clothing present.

Everyone had been shocked by this discovery, none more so than Lavelle, his birthday celebrations well and truly ruined. He had spent much of the immediate aftermath in something of a daze. He remembered helping the retired doctor to further unwrap the corpse, and then doing his best to try and reassure his guests, apologising to some and consoling others. It was only as they were preparing to leave that, with Hardwick's help, he managed to get them to promise that they would leak none of this to the authorities. The last thing the Order was needing was for something as serious and as blighting as this to be made common knowledge. It had been Hardwick who had reinforced this position by stating that if the police were brought in, everyone there would be subjected to the most rigorous and awkward questioning as to why they were there in the first place, well aware that what they were doing bordered on the illegal.

'So just what the hell are we going to do about it?' asked Lavelle. He felt sick and his pale face was drawn. Gone now was the calm and self-assured man who had presided over the evening's previous events. 'It's not as if he can stay here, stinking up my study.'

'Well, like I said, the last thing we should do is contact the police. That would be disastrous — both for you personally and for the Order. The less they know about it the better.' Hardwick took a sip from his coffee.

'But surely a crime's been committed

here?' said Williams. He was a tall man, smartly dressed with a well-groomed beard. 'It's our duty to report it. By failing to do so, won't we be accessories to murder or something? I don't fancy a ten-year stretch in prison for something I didn't do. I've got a reputation to protect.'

'That's exactly why we can't go to the police,' replied Hardwick sternly. 'Just think things through for a moment, won't you? As an academic, you've probably got the most to lose if news of this gets around. A couple of years back UNESCO made a law prohibiting and preventing the illicit import, export and transfer of rare antiquities. Something tells me the authorities aren't going to be too pleased to find out that we were about to cut up a mummy.'

'So we come back to the same question — what do we do?' asked Lavelle. He was now well out of his depth. While everything had been all about Ancient Egypt he had been in charge, having been in what psychologists commonly referred to as his 'comfort zone'. Now, unable to fully deal with the situation, he had relinquished leadership, letting others take over.

'We could just get rid of it,' suggested Braithwaite. 'Burn it . . . or take it out to a field and bury it. Cover it up and forget about it. Nobody'll ever know.'

'It's a solution to the problem, I suppose,' agreed Lavelle. He had been thinking along similar lines.

'I'd have thought the main issue was surely one of establishing the dead man's identity and then trying to work out exactly how he ended up where he did.' Williams took his pipe from his mouth and tapped out the smouldering contents in the bowl. 'It would seem logical to me that whoever murdered this man was probably one and the same as the man who sold it to you in the first place.'

Lavelle and Hardwick exchanged glances.

'But surely if you were going to dispose of a body you'd find a better way of doing it than this?' said Braithwaite. 'I mean, it's like something from one of my stories. Admittedly, he hasn't come back to life and killed us all, but surely only a truly twisted individual would come up with such a plan as this?'

'You've been very reluctant about telling us where exactly you got it,' said Hoffman. 'I think now's the time to come clean. I mean, even if the murder of this man is of no consequence to you, I'd have thought — not wanting to sound crass — that you'd be angry at having been fobbed off as it were.'

Lavelle was beginning to feel as though he was being subjected to an interrogation. For a fleeting moment reality seemed to slip away. Perhaps this was nothing but a nightmare, one from which he would awake in the morning. Wiping a sheen of sweat from his forehead, he shifted uncomfortably in his chair.

'I bought what I thought was the mummy some three months ago from a Mr Rupert Snell, a reclusive circus owner with something of a reputation when it comes to acquiring illicit archaeological artefacts. He assured me that the coffin was authentic and that it had been in his family for many years, one of his ancestors having been a close friend of

Giovanni Belzoni. Of course, I demanded to have a look at it for myself, to which he readily agreed. Taking some of my books, I drove out to his home in order to study the sarcophagus and ascertain its authenticity. I asked several questions pertaining to its provenance, age and contents, which Snell answered to the best of his knowledge. Having met the man, I don't think that he'd be the type to commit murder. For starters, he must be in his seventies.'

Sitting back, arms crossed over his chest, Williams said: 'I fully take on board everything that's been said, but even so I still think we *have* to get the police involved. There *has* to be a proper investigation into this. Whoever this murdered individual is, he would undoubtedly have had family — parents, maybe a wife and kids. Think of that.'

Hardwick shook his head. 'It would be professional suicide if we dragged the authorities into this. However, there may be . . . other ways.'

'Just what are you talking about?' inquired Williams.

'I didn't get to where I am today by keeping my nose clean,' admitted Hardwick. 'I've had occasion to resort to a little blackmail. Just for leverage, you understand. To this end, I keep a certain private investigator on my books. His name's Adam Blake and he's both professional and extremely discreet. If anyone can throw some light on this, I'm sure he can. No doubt he's working on another case at the moment, but I'll try and find him tomorrow evening. In the meantime, I suggest that we don't do anything to draw attention to this.'

★   ★   ★

'The Pit' was a hell-hole: a squalid, smoky, subterranean madhouse beneath a disused cinema. It was here in this underground vault that illegal bare-knuckle boxing bouts took place. On fight nights, it was invariably filled with a riotous throng of angry, foul-mouthed, unpleasant-looking men, all eager to place their bets and witness the primitive spectacle of bare-chested bruisers battering the living daylights out of each other in a place where the Queensberry Rules were unheard of and where the bloodier the better was the order of the day.

There was an overwhelming, threatening atmosphere to the Pit that, along with the pervasive stink of sweat, blood and cheap liquor, made it downright nasty. Men cursed volubly, drank, jostled, smoked and fought, seeking their cheap and dubious entertainment any way they could, whilst the activities in the makeshift ring — little more than a sawdust-covered clearing — often bordered on the murderous.

The fights were largely unsupervised, and with no real referee to intervene, they soon descended into no-holds-barred brutality, the winner being the one who succeeded in pummelling his opponent unconscious. The only solid rules were no weapons, no kicking, and no eye-gouging or hair-pulling, but apart from that anything else was acceptable so long as it involved a lot of violence. Even when a combatant deviated from the few rules there were, it usually went unnoticed.

'So what exactly is it I should be looking out for?' Adam Blake scanned the crowd from where he and Benny McGuire stood on a raised grill-work platform close to the stairs. Most of those he could see were no doubt 'travelling folk' who had come to back their home-grown champions, but there were one or two faces he thought he recognised. 'And what is it you suspect? Drug-taking? Match-fixing?'

McGuire turned to face Blake. 'Christ knows. Besides, that's what you're being paid to find out. There's definitely something going on though.' He was a big stocky Irishman with a broad ruddy face, his squashed nose and missing front teeth evidence of his past experience in the ring — a time which had earned him the epithet 'Butcher'. His breath reeked of cheap whisky. 'There'll be a few fights before Keegan comes out.'

'Is this a normal turnout?' asked Blake.

'There's a big crowd in from Maccles-field this evening. They've all come to see their local boy, Heinrich Maul, take on Keegan.' McGuire shook his head.

'They'll all be going home disappointed, I'll tell you that. As for Maul, well . . . he'll be lucky if he gets out of here alive.'

Blake smiled wryly. 'Heinrich Maul? Sure sounds like a local boy.'

'That's just his boxing name. I think his real name's Henry Mole. As I told you earlier, on paper he's far better than Keegan. An unbeaten record. He's massive — a true monster.'

Below them the crowd roared as one. The noise was almost deafening.

Spotlights fell on a shadowy opening as the first of the evening's pugilists stepped out. Surrounded by his promoter and some of his fans, the scrawny blond-haired fist-fighter strutted for the audience. Throwing a few practice jabs, he made his way into the clearing.

'Who's that?' Blake had not heard the boxer's name announced.

'That's 'Pretty Boy' Stanley. A real ladies' man. He's got a good punch but he's been knocked out more times than I can remember. Too much of a showman, if you know what I mean.'

The spotlight panned over to another entrance and Stanley's opponent came forth — a hulking black man with cropped hair and a wild, staring look.

McGuire laughed. 'And this is Rex Hodges. He's an animal. Saw him kill a man a year or so back. Took six others to get him off the poor bastard. He just went berserk. Pounded the guy into the ground. Stomped all over his head. It was a hell of a mess.'

Blake was unsure how to respond to that. As a private investigator he had dealt with more than his share of unsavoury individuals and had been in several truly inhospitable places, but this dreadful arena with these lawless, violent men was undoubtedly the worst. There was danger here all around, and not just for those about to fight. He was only too aware of the hostile stares levelled at him, and he was under no illusions that it was only because he was in the company of McGuire that none had, as yet, made a move against him.

A fat, sweating man in a crumpled suit wearing a black-and-white striped tie announced both fighters. A bell sounded and what followed was four minutes of pounding, bone-jarring violence which culminated in Stanley being carried off by two of his supporters, blood streaming from his broken nose. The fat man raised Hodges's arm in the air and proclaimed him the victor. The black boxer was just leaving when he, too, collapsed and had to be taken away.

Two more fights followed: savage, bloody affairs that astounded Blake. Not so much in terms of their ferocity, but as in just how much pain and suffering a man could take before succumbing to it all. The last of the two bouts went on for almost fifteen minutes as the evenly matched combatants exchanged bone-crunching blows, slogging it out, blood and sweat spraying with every punch. Both were battered black and blue, their ribs and faces covered in bruised weals. Each man's eyes were puffed and bleeding. With the realisation that neither man had the strength remaining to continue, in the end it was declared a draw.

The baying mob cried out for more. They were becoming unruly. Voices were raised and a bottle was thrown. A scuffle broke out between a group of loud-mouths at the rear of the crowd.

McGuire patted Blake on the shoulder, untroubled by the anarchy below, obviously considering it a normal occurrence. 'Keegan's up next. Keep an eye on Musgrove, his promoter and trainer.'

Blake nodded, awaiting the arrival of the next fighter.

After a few minutes the crowd parted as, accompanied by much cheering, a giant brute wearing an SS death's-head cap bulldozed his way forward. Bare-chested like the others, and covered in swastika tattoos, he stood a good head and a half above those surrounding him. His face was more or less flat, making it look as though he had either fallen on his face from a considerable height or been struck hard by a shovel. Sweat glistened off his heavily muscled torso. He removed his cap, revealing his bald head, and began snarling like a chained beast.

'As you've probably guessed, that's

Maul,' said McGuire, raising his voice so that Blake could hear him. 'He's the current North-East Champion. A true legend, despite the fact that he's as mad as a meat-axe, having taken too many bangs to the head. Fought him myself several years back.' With a heavily callused hand, he brushed his scurf-speckled hair aside and pointed to his missing lower left ear. 'Bastard did this to me. Still, I gave him as good as I got.'

Yelling insults to the crowd, Maul stomped angrily about; making threats, informing everyone, in no uncertain terms, just what he was going to do to Keegan. His supporters — the mob from Macclesfield — went wild.

The spotlight panned over to one side.

With a deafening blare, someone let off a klaxon.

Weaving through the crowds came a wiry, dark-haired man and two of his attendants.

'Here's Keegan,' announced McGuire.

Blake fixed his eyes on the scrawny boxer. He looked like a nine stone weakling who had never seen the inside of a training gym never mind a fighting ring. He had some muscle but compared to Maul he was a gnat, ready to be squashed. This was going to be one hell of a one-sided contest, he thought. 'Christ! He doesn't stand a chance.'

'You just wait. The weird-looking guy on his right's Musgrove,' revealed McGuire.

Menacingly cracking his knuckles, Maul sneered as Keegan entered the clearing. He then moved forward.

The smaller man went to meet him.

Unless by some miracle Keegan was able to pull off a true David versus Goliath, Blake guessed the smaller boxer would probably be leaving here comatose, on a stretcher, every bone in his body broken — and that was if he was lucky. He knew that speed and agility might be in the shorter man's favour but even so this was as mismatched a fight as he had ever seen — a featherweight against a heavyweight. It was almost perverse sending two such unevenly sized fighters against one another.

The fat man in the suit was about to officially open the fight when Maul lashed out with a meaty right fist which struck Keegan full in the face, knocking him backwards, spinning him into the riotous crowd. With a berserk savagery he leapt forward, fiercely pushing aside the officiator who had tried to intervene.

'He'll regret that,' muttered McGuire.

The Irishman proved to be correct with his prediction, for in the next instant Keegan was pushed back into the ring, whereupon he let fly with a rapid series of lefts and rights that smote into the larger man's torso. Blake could hear the sickening crunch of ribs being broken.

Maul screamed and staggered back, his face contorting into a grimace of absolute agony. Still Keegan pummelled into him, his punches becoming faster until they became blurs that were painful on the eye. These were no mere jabs intent on loosening up and weakening an opponent — these were tight-fisted killer punches, each one sending a visible shockwave which rippled through Maul.

The huge neo-Nazi was getting pulverized.

Hands on the railing, McGuire leaned

out further, scrutinising the action, trying to make out for himself just how Keegan was winning.

Blake felt a sudden tap on his shoulder. He turned and was surprised to see his main employer, Don Hardwick. Without a word said, the rich American handed across a slip of paper and then turned away.

'*Did you see that?*' asked McGuire excitedly, having just witnessed Maul get knocked to the ground. There was no doubt the large man had taken a severe pummelling, but he had seen him take far worse. It was clear, to him at least, that this was all a farce. 'I'm sure that this has all been put on. It's a set-up. A fix.' He turned to the private investigator. 'You saw that, didn't you?'

'Why . . . yes, I think you're right,' Blake mumbled, unsure as to just what the other was talking about, his attention having been diverted by Hardwick. He had only taken on this job for McGuire to make some quick money; but now that his boss had need of his services, he was more than prepared to abandon this

41

particular investigation.

'So you agree?'

'Yeah . . . sure. Look, I've got to go make a quick phone call. I'll be back shortly.' Blake turned and walked away from the confused Irishman. Hoping that he would catch up with Hardwick, he quickened his pace, making his way into the dimly lit foyer area. There was no one to be seen. Walking over to one of the wall lights, he removed the note which the other had given him and read: *Tanis Towers — tomorrow morning, nine o'clock.*

3

It was raining quite heavily as Blake drove along the gravel driveway which led up to Tanis Towers. He knew there would no doubt be repercussions for having abandoned McGuire's case, but his true loyalty had always been with Hardwick, whose car he could see parked over to one side. The house was a large, rambling Victorian affair set within its own grounds and clearly the residence of someone with a considerable amount of money.

He parked up, left the car and made a dash for the front door, knocking loudly on it twice. It was opened by a tall grey-haired man. Unshaven and with bloodshot eyes, there was a weary and somewhat dishevelled look about him.

'Adam Blake. I've an appointment to meet Don Hardwick.'

'Yes, we were expecting you. I'm Jeremy Lavelle. Pleased to meet you. Come on in.'

Blake stepped inside. He took off his damp coat and hung it up on a hook in the hallway.

'Please, if you'd follow me.'

'It's some place you've got here, Mr Lavelle. The kind of house I'd like to own some day. Are these real?' asked Blake as they went down the corridor, which was decorated with countless pieces of replica ancient Egyptian artwork. He knew next to nothing about ancient history but he was fascinated all the same.

'Well . . . yes, in fact,' Lavelle lied. He was about to say something else when a door opened.

'There you are, Blake.' Hardwick looked pointedly at his wristwatch. 'You're ten minutes late.'

The private investigator gave a non-committal shrug of his shoulders. 'Blame the traffic. Besides, you could've given me more to go by than just the name of this place. It took me some time to find.'

'Oh, come now. A man of your means.' Hardwick stepped aside, gesturing for Blake to enter the room. He then went over and sat down at a large oak desk.

'This is Charles Braithwaite, and Mr Lavelle you've just met.' Braithwaite nodded to Blake from his seat near the desk.

The two of them went inside, Lavelle closing the door behind him. He then went over and sat beside Hardwick.

'So what seems to be the problem?' asked Blake, sitting down. 'And before you start, you do realise that I've had to forsake a case that I was already on? It's not as though I was paid much up front, but the man I was working for didn't strike me as the kind of guy I'd want to get on the wrong side of.'

'Be that as it may, I can assure you that you'll be very well paid for helping us out,' replied Hardwick. 'In fact, if you do this well, I might even double your normal fee.'

'Sounds interesting . . . so why don't you tell me what this is all about? Just what is it you want me to look into?'

Over the next twenty minutes Hardwick explained all that had happened, telling Blake that the corpse was still in situ within its wooden casket in Lavelle's study.

45

The private investigator had listened attentively throughout, making the occasional note on a pad of paper. 'Given the circumstances, I fully understand why you didn't want to get the police involved. I must admit this has to be one of the most bizarre cases I've ever been asked to look into. That said, it sounds interesting.'

'So what do you think? Do you think this Rupert Snell character murdered someone and then decided to make him up as a mummy in order to foist him off on Mr Lavelle?' asked Hardwick. 'If so, it's a pretty ingenious and unique way of disposing of a victim.'

'In addition to a profitable way of doing so,' added Lavelle. 'I paid the best part of a thousand pounds for it.'

'And I take it you didn't get a receipt?' quipped Blake.

'Why, of course not. We merely made a gentleman's agreement and I bought it in good faith,' Lavelle answered.

'A classic case of a pig in a poke,' said Braithwaite.

'I take it that when you bought this mummy from Snell, you didn't tell him

46

that you planned to unwrap it?' asked Blake.

Lavelle shook his head. 'I can't remember. I don't think so. Why do you ask?'

'Well, if Snell was of the opinion that all you wanted to do was display the unopened coffin, or at the most open it up but not unwrap the mummy . . . then it would suggest to me that he may've believed that you were in effect providing him with a pretty good opportunity of concealing a body.

'That assumes that it was Snell who killed this man,' said Braithwaite.

'It does, but that isn't necessarily so. It could be that he was the one who came up with the idea.' Blake interlaced his fingers and sat back in his chair. 'Then again, he could be completely innocent — ignorant of the whole thing.'

'That's unlikely, isn't it?' Hardwick removed a cigarette from a packet, lit it with a gold lighter and took a deep drag. Blowing smoke from his nostrils, he added: 'I don't see how he can possibly not be responsible.'

Lavelle, who had been thinking things over, thought that he had some idea as to what Blake was inferring. 'I suppose it's remotely possible that someone other than Snell placed the wrapped-up body inside, switching it with the genuine mummy.'

'A bit far-fetched, don't you think?' Hardwick was doubtful.

'Admittedly, but it's something we shouldn't rule out.' Having missed his breakfast in order to make this early morning appointment, Blake reached over to the plate of biscuits Lavelle had provided and helped himself to a handful of digestives. 'You say that he's stabbed and beheaded? Do we have anything else to go on — such as how long he's been dead, or whether there are any clues on his articles of clothing?'

'We checked his pockets. Nothing. As for the body itself, well, apart from the obvious puncture wounds to the stomach there doesn't seem to be much else to go on. Perhaps if we had access to a professional pathologist who had no qualms about performing an unsanctioned autopsy . . . '

Hardwick stared coldly at Blake.

Blake finished off one of the biscuits. 'Okay, I get your point.'

'No doubt you'll be wanting to take a look at the stiff,' said Braithwaite.

'Yes. Although I doubt whether I'll be able to learn anything new from it.' Blake rose from his chair. 'Well, I guess there's no time like the present. Besides, I'd probably rather have a look before lunch, if you get my meaning.'

Lavelle got to his feet. 'If you'll follow me.' He led the way to the study and pushed wide the door. As he had neither the time nor the inclination to tidy up, the room retained its tomb-like appearance.

'Bloody hell!' commented Blake, taking in his surroundings. 'I feel as though I've gone back in time. Bet this must have taken some effort to set up.' Wincing a little from the smell which Lavelle had tried to mask with pungent air freshener, he walked over to join the other who stood by the wooden sarcophagus. He frowned as he gazed upon its gruesome contents.

'Not very pretty, is it?' he commented.

'I take it you've seen a dead body before?'

'Twice.'

When Blake failed to elaborate, Lavelle went on: 'Well as you can see he's not only headless but he's also been stabbed, three times. The mummy's head is quite probably real.'

'I wonder what he did for a living? He's slightly built, so that may rule out any kind of hard manual labour. In fact, anyone bigger and I doubt they'd have fitted inside this box. What would you guess — ten, eleven stone?' Blake could see Hardwick standing in the doorway. No doubt he had had enough of the stink and did not want to enter any further.

'About that,' Lavelle agreed.

'You mentioned that this Snell character ran a circus. Do you think this dead man could've been an acrobat or something similar?' Blake continued to examine the body. 'I'm just going on this guy's physical dimensions.'

'I guess it's possible.'

'*Acrobat?* He could just've easily have been a skinny doctor . . . or a malnourished high-court judge,' said Hardwick

50

unhelpfully. He had a point all the same.

'True enough,' Blake conceded. 'I was just going on the circus angle.' Having now seen enough of the reeking cadaver, he went and joined his employer. 'I think my first line of inquiry has to be Snell. See if I can find out any more about this corpse.'

'I can give you an address,' said Lavelle, lowering the lid on the casket. 'What's more, I'd like to come with you. I want to look him in the eye and hear his explanation for all this. He lives way out in the country, miles from anywhere.'

★ ★ ★

It was approaching midday when Blake and Lavelle got out of the former's car and stood before the large black barn conversion which was set within a somewhat neglected garden. It was still raining and a grey dreariness hung over everything. Two huge willow trees, their leaves piled all around, their fallen branches scattered on the lawn, stood like gaunt sentinels on either side of the wooden building.

'Is this it?' asked Blake, staring unimpressed at the rundown property. Aside from his own car, there were no other vehicles in the driveway and the whole place looked deserted. The nearest house was half a mile away and that had looked just as abandoned.

Lavelle had to think about it for a moment. 'Yes . . . I think so.' It was hard to be certain, for the place was now but a shadow of its former self. Admittedly, he remembered the garden had been in a bit of a mess when he had come out here several months back, but the barn itself had been well maintained. Now he could see two smashed windows.

'Come on. Let's see if anybody's in.' Leading the way, Blake headed for the front door. Under different circumstances, perhaps with a bit of sunshine and a spot of refurbishing, the barn would have looked quite habitable, he thought. However, given its current decrepit state, it was more of an eyesore. Reaching the door, he gave three loud knocks. Twenty or so seconds later when there was no reply, he knocked again.

'Looks like this has been a wasted trip,' said Lavelle.

Blake tried the door and was not too surprised to find it locked. Suddenly, he caught a flash of movement beyond the large ground-floor windows. 'There's someone inside.' Next came the sound of a back door opening, and then he was sprinting to his left. Dashing round the corner of the building, he caught sight of a dark-haired man running away. 'Get back here!' he shouted as he gave chase, aware that Lavelle was struggling to keep up.

The rear garden extended much further than the front — a length of leaf-covered lawn that stretched for fifty yards. At the far end was a barbed-wire fence which the mysterious figure was now frantically trying to disentangle himself from. Snaring long lengths of his black jumper, he pulled himself free and was just about to start off again when he tripped, his feet slipping in the clinging mud which covered the ground. With a curse, he pulled himself to his feet.

Emitting a savage cry, Blake reached over the fence and grabbed the man by the collar. He pulled hard, attempting to draw him back through the widened fence. A barb tore at his hand, instantly drawing blood and forcing him to bite down the pain.

'Get off me, you bastard!' the man cursed. He began shaking, trying desperately to break free from Blake's hold.

Blake tightened his grip. It was an awkward position to be in and he knew that his hold on the other was precarious to say the least. Had there not been the obstacle between the two, he could have forced the man to the ground; but as it was he had no real purchase. If the other were to prove the stronger it would be he who would be dragged into the barbed wire fence. Thus it was with some relief that he heard Lavelle panting breathlessly behind him.

'Get your filthy hands off me!'

'My friend's got a gun,' Blake lied. 'If you don't fancy getting shot, you'd better stop struggling.'

'All right. Don't shoot, for God's sake!'

All of the fight was suddenly knocked out of the man. He raised his arms and slowly turned round.

Blake was surprised to see how young he was. Twenty-five, if that; his skin was sallow and there was an unhealthy look to his face. He parted the barbed wire, holding it open so that the young man could climb back through.

Ducking his head, he did just that. 'Are you the police?' he asked. There was an element of fear in his voice. It was obvious that he had been caught doing something wrong; and what was more, he knew it.

'Who are you?' Blake asked, grabbing the young man by the sleeve to ensure he did not make another break for it. 'And where's Snell — the owner of this house?'

'The name's . . . Martin.'

'Martin what?'

'Martin' hesitated. He was either unsure of his surname or else he was rapidly thinking one up. 'Eh, Jennings.'

'Sure, and we're Laurel and Hardy,' argued Blake.

'Honest.' 'Jennings' — if that was

indeed his real name — glanced furtively around. 'As to the owner . . . I'm the owner. I've never heard of this Snell guy before.'

'You're lying. I can see it in your eyes.' In fact the only thing Blake could see in the man's eyes was a bloodshot blankness indicative of someone on drugs. 'So come on, tell us — where's Snell?'

'I'm telling you I've never heard of him.'

'So how long have you lived here?' asked Lavelle. He had not prepared himself for these riotous antics and he was feeling more than a little uncomfortable with the whole thing. Was it possible that they had come to the wrong address? In which case, were he and Blake not drastically overstepping the law — chasing and threatening some poor innocent? Could it be that the young man had chosen to flee suspecting he and the private investigator were thieves or worse? He had read in the papers that there was quite a lot of crime reported in these rural areas.

'A couple of weeks or so.' Despite his

glazed eyes, 'Jennings' looked scared. 'Look, all right, I'll tell you the truth. My real name's Matthew Jennings. I've been squatting here for the past couple of weeks. Snell's dead.'

Blake straightened. 'What?'

'Snell — the man who used to live here. He died shortly before I moved in.'

'This had better not be another lie,' warned Blake. He threw Lavelle a swift glance, noting the puzzled, almost disbelieving look on his face.

Jennings shook his head. 'Do you think I've been staying here with his blessing? That bastard wouldn't have put up with that.'

'So you knew him, did you?' asked Blake. This was beginning to get interesting.

'Yeah, I knew him all right. I worked for him. I take it you know he ran a small circus outfit? Well, I used to be one of the roustabouts who helped in setting it up. Anyway, what exactly is it you guys are after? I'm coming to the conclusion that you ain't the police. So what is it? If he owed you money — '

'You're right, we're not the police,' interrupted Blake. 'However, there are certain things that we want to find out. And if Snell's dead, then discovering them isn't going to prove easy.' Having disclosed the fact that they were not there in any kind of legal capacity, and by doing so it was less likely that the young man would try to escape, he relinquished his hold. 'Now then, tell us exactly what happened to Snell. How did he die?'

'I'm not sure. I know there was talk in the village that thieves broke into his house. Whether they killed him, I don't know. To be honest, I thought that was what you were when I saw you snooping around the place. I thought you were casing the joint, so to speak.'

'Well, we're not thieves. Come on, let's go inside, shall we?'

'Okay,' answered Jennings. 'But you'll find nothing of any help in there. The place is a tip.'

Blake grinned. 'We'll see.'

★ ★ ★

There was more to the chaotic mess inside than just general untidiness and the lack of proper habitation. To Blake's trained eye it was fairly clear that, at some time in the past, the place had been thoroughly ransacked and that it had been done by a person, or more likely persons, in search of something. For what to the layman's eye appeared to be just a haphazard, disorganised distribution of rubbish and a seemingly random placement of overturned furniture and the like indicated to him the methodical, if somewhat rushed, rifling of the place. For the main, it seemed that Jennings, whose small sleeping and cooking area was thankfully confined to one side room at the rear, had not infringed elsewhere; thus there was little to no contamination of what was, in Blake's opinion, a crime scene — admittedly one that was at least several weeks old, but a crime scene nonetheless.

'I'd a feeling that Snell didn't have any family or much in the way of friends, but I'd have thought that someone would've come to check on his property after he'd died,' said Lavelle. 'Surely the authorities would've been informed?'

'I guess that depends.' Blake was only half-listening, temporarily preoccupied with going through a heap of old books. From past experience he knew that important snippets of information were sometimes to be found tucked away inside their pages.

'Look, I don't know what you two are after, but if we can come to some kind of an arrangement I might be able to help you out,' announced Jennings from where he sat, eating from a packet of cold sausage rolls. 'I mean, if you were to keep quiet about me being here and all, I'll let you into a secret.'

'Okay, let's hear it,' said Lavelle.

'You promise not to tell anyone that I'm here?'

'Sure, we promise,' agreed Blake insincerely. 'Now what's this secret of yours?' He doubted whether or not it would be of any significance, but it would do no harm in finding out just what it was.

Jennings paused for a moment. Rubbing away a mound of crumbs from his ratty jumper, he gave a conspiratorial look about. 'It must have been back in mid-August. As I told you, I did a stint as a hired hand at Snell's circus. One day I overheard a conversation that I don't think I was meant to hear.'

The young man now had Blake's attention. 'Go on,' he prompted with a nod of his head.

'Whenever Snell was on site he stayed in a big tent, really grand. I was going to ask him something — I think it was to do with the ticket booth — when I heard angry voices coming from inside. Now, it wasn't that unknown for one of the performers to get pissed off with how they were being treated, or even for a punter to turn up demanding a refund or some such. But I could tell immediately that this was something different. Creeping closer, I heard one guy threatening Snell. Something got broken, a bottle or a mirror, I guess.'

'This is all rather vague,' said Blake. 'What were they talking about?'

'I can't remember it word for word, but it definitely had something to do with money . . . and Egypt of all places. The guy that was shouting at Snell was really angry. He said something about telling everybody just what it was that Snell was up to. I guess he was making blackmail threats towards him. Now, I don't know if Snell was involved in anything criminal or not, but to be honest I wouldn't put it past him. There was talk that he could get hold of things — you know, illegal things — and sell them on.'

Lavelle gave Blake a knowing look. 'Did you see this man at all?' asked the private investigator.

'Only for a moment.' Jennings reached into a trouser pocket and removed a stick of chewing gum, which he put into his mouth. 'Short, with black hair and a moustache. Certainly not one of the regular circus workers whom I had come to know.'

'Was it just him?' inquired Blake.

Jennings nodded. 'Apart from Snell, he was the only one I saw coming out of the tent.'

'This is getting stranger,' said Lavelle. He turned to Blake. 'Do you think that this mystery man may've killed Snell? In which case, could he be the same person who . . . ?' He stopped himself, unwilling to relate the mystery of the corpse in the sarcophagus to Jennings. After all, there was no telling what level of involvement Jennings had had in this, if any. All that he had just told them could be nothing more than a complete pack of lies; a bargaining chip used to persuade them not to inform the authorities of his presence in Snell's house.

'It's hard to say. Later, I'm going to do a little research. See if I can establish Snell's true cause of death. Shouldn't be too difficult.' Blake went back to his rummaging.

For the next forty-five minutes, the two of them searched the converted barn for anything that might prove useful. Jennings kept a low profile throughout, his offer to help look for anything that might be of importance turned down by Blake. There was plenty of information to be found concerning Snell's dodgy dealings: clearly falsified documents pertaining to animal welfare at his circus and even reference to a few bullying letters sent to various landowners, but nothing crucial; nothing which gave a firm lead for the next line of inquiry. They did, however, unearth a box of old circus pamphlets, on the back of which was a grainy photograph of Snell's cheery, avuncular face.

'I don't think we're going to find anything here,' commented Lavelle, waiting until Jennings had gone to the toilet. 'I think if there was anything relating to the murder of our friend in the sarcophagus, it's now long gone.'

Blake was becoming exasperated. He prided himself on being able to find that which had either been hidden purposefully or which others thought insignificant, but which he knew was of importance. He had scoured through the usual places: the sole filing cabinet, the boxes under the bed, along the numerous shelves crammed with old paperbacks, and even in the garden shed. Nothing. It seemed that there were no clues here. With a resigned sigh, he threw away the last of the letters he had been going through and turned to face Lavelle. 'Let's look at the facts again. When was the first time you came here?'

Lavelle thought the question over for a moment. 'I'd say it was about — '

'I want an exact date.'

Lavelle thought harder. He looked towards the huge beams which supported the ceiling and cupped his chin. 'I can't remember the exact date.'

'Don't you keep a diary?'

'No,' answered Lavelle, shaking his head.

'Well, think.

'I'm pretty sure it was a weekday in early August. Possibly the eighth or the ninth. For some reason I'm thinking it was a Tuesday.'

Blake removed a diary from an inner jacket pocket, consulted it and scribbled something inside with a pen. 'Okay, that makes it the eighth. Now, if we can establish when Snell died, then — '

'I don't know when he died, but I know he was buried on the eleventh — Remembrance Day. I remember because there was some uproar in the village when the hearse which carried him disrupted the memorial service,' revealed a voice behind them.

They both turned. Neither had heard

Jennings approach.

'You'd better not have been eavesdropping,' said Blake coldly.

'Of course not . . . I overheard you. There's a difference.

Blake shook his head in annoyance. The last thing he wanted was for this newly met individual to start acting the amateur sleuth. 'Believe me, it would be in your best interest to stay out of this. I appreciate your situation and I, for one, have no problem about you squatting here on a temporary basis, but take my advice and stay out of things.' Realising that there was little more to be found at this address, he headed for the main door, gesturing for Lavelle to follow.

4

A late autumnal evening darkness had fallen on Tanis Towers.

Through a contact at the police station, Blake had succeeded in getting hold of the official police report relating to the circus owner's death. He relayed the facts to Hardwick and Lavelle. 'Snell's body was discovered by the milkman early on the morning of Saturday, November third. He was found lying just outside his front door. He'd been decapitated and, as far as I'm aware, his head's still missing. In addition, as we've seen for ourselves, the property had been broken into. There were no witnesses to the murder and as yet there have been no arrests, although the police are pursuing several lines of inquiry. Which, from my experience, means they haven't got a clue as to who's responsible. However, they haven't ruled out the possibility that it was connected in some way with Snell's murky past.'

'Maybe we should just forget about this whole thing,' suggested Lavelle. Not for the first time, he was feeling uncomfortable with this turn of events. There were now two deaths and, as far as he was concerned, it was high time to disengage from things before they became even more dangerous. He now regretted ever getting involved with Snell. He should have stuck to his original fiftieth birthday plan, which was to hire one of the ancient Egyptian galleries at the British Museum for the evening. 'After all, the only person who could've explained matters is now dead.'

'That's a defeatist and short-sighted attitude,' said Hardwick. He was standing with his back to the fire, a glass of bourbon in his hand. 'No one exists without links to other people, and this man Snell must've had more links than most. As a circus organiser, he'll have known people up and down the country and quite likely abroad as well. Someone foisted that body off on you. We don't know why yet, but they may've had personal reasons for it. What I'm saying is, you may've been specifically targeted.'

'I hardly think that'd be the case. What would be the point?' Despite his words, Lavelle looked extremely troubled by this possibility.

'Well, I know that the Order's ruffled a few feathers over the years; academic feathers for the most part. Could be that someone decided to play a trick on us.'

'*A trick!?* For God's sake, Don — you don't kill someone, chop off their head and wrap them up as a mummy to set up a practical joke!' Lavelle exclaimed.

Hardwick merely shrugged his shoulders, 'It's a bit far-fetched, I know, but the fact remains: you've been landed with an almighty problem, and it doesn't feel accidental to me.' He turned to Blake and pointed a finger. 'I want you to start making enquiries among the circus folk. Find out if Snell had a second-in-command. Find out where they toured. In particular, find someone who hated Snell and will tell you any rumours there may've been. You know dirt when you see it, so get digging.'

Blake nodded his acceptance of the

orders. 'What have you done with the body?' he asked.

'I've made arrangements for it to be kept on ice, literally, for the moment,' Hardwick said. His tone of voice discouraged further questioning and Blake took the hint.

'Okay. I'll go back and talk to that guy we found at Snell's house. He should have a lead for the circus people. I'll also go back through the missing persons lists, see if anything matches our stiff.' Blake looked at Lavelle. 'I'd also like a list of any people or organisations you think might have it in for you. Mr Hardwick's right to raise the possibility of this being an attack on you. Although if it was, I'd expect you to find this dragged out into the open. If someone's trying to discredit you, there's no point in doing it behind closed doors. If the police come round following up an anonymous tip-off, that'd tell us a lot.'

'Oh, God!' Lavelle put his head in his hands. 'I don't think I can cope with this.'

Hardwick finished his drink and picked up his coat. 'If that happens, you call me at once, Jeremy. I can guarantee that no one who was present at the unwrapping will talk. I've done a bit of ringing round and amazingly all they remember of your party was a blow-out meal and too much drink. It's not in any of our interests to have the Order dragged through the courts. Those idiots who can't countenance anything off the beaten track would have a field day, and I'm not having that.' He was grimly determined.

'Thanks, Don. I don't know what I'd do without you,' Lavelle said, looking a little reassured but still jittery.

'Don't sweat it. I'll get this sorted out. Come on, Blake. Time to go.'

When Lavelle had seen them out, Hardwick walked with the private investigator to their cars. 'See what you can find on Snell, but I want you to do some background on Lavelle too.'

'What's the angle?' Blake asked, not entirely surprised by the request.

'He's brilliant of course, but he's put some noses out of joint with his revelations. I know some professor at Oxford rubbished him last year and the

E.E.S. hate his guts.'

'E.E.S.?'

'The Egypt Exploration Society,' Hardwick explained. 'A bunch of stuck-up, narrow-minded, self-important fools. They think they know it all, but in truth they know nothing.'

Blake was taken aback by the vehemence with which his employer said this. The man was practically snarling.

'Okay. I'll do a search for potential enemies. If one of them turns out to have a link with Snell or his circus, that could be what we're looking for.' He leaned to open his car door but Hardwick put his hand on it, making him pause.

'One more thing. If you do turn up anything nasty, don't tell Lavelle. He'd go to pieces. Report it to me and I'll take care of it.' Hardwick moved away to his own car. He owned several, but the one he was currently using was a black Ford Zephyr that Blake coveted. 'I'll get some money sent over to you in the morning for expenses. I want this resolved quickly.'

'When did you ever want anything done slowly?' Blake muttered, watching the car pull away. Still, it was an interesting case. He usually got mundane jobs from Hardwick — credit checks, tracking down people who had defaulted on loans, digging up dirt on business rivals and that sort of stuff. This was more the kind of thing he had become a private investigator for, although he never would have dreamed he would be faced with a headless body and a bodiless head.

* * *

The narrow stairs up to Blake's office were only lit by the orange glow of the streetlight conveniently placed outside the stairwell window. It saved him from buying bulbs for the bare fitting that had been there when he moved in. Climbing the stairs, with the facts of the case circling in his mind, he automatically checked that no one had been there in his absence. The door that led to his office was kept locked, so in theory no one could be there without his invitation, but it did not hurt to be both paranoid and suspicious.

Satisfied that nothing was out of place, he opened the door and turned on the light, illuminating the dingy room with his desk in the middle and a couple of filing cabinets against the walls. There was a second door which led to a smaller room with a sink, a kettle and a battered leather sofa. Until a few months ago he had used this to get some sleep before all-night surveillance jobs, preferring to keep away from his flat during the day. It had helped to have a separate home, to keep somewhere different to go at the end of the day's work. That had changed when his landlord had put up the rent on his flat. The investigative jobs had been thin on the ground and he been forced to admit to himself that he could no longer afford two places — so the flat had to go.

It was far from ideal. For a start, his office shared a toilet with the fish and chip shop downstairs, and there was no bathroom. He got round this by using the local swimming pool's amenities, but it was not the same. More worryingly, only having one bolt-hole made him too easy to find.

Dumping his car keys on the desk, Blake sat down and started to make notes. If he did well on this case for Hardwick he might make enough money to get himself another place, at least for a while. At the age of forty-seven, he was getting too old to be sleeping on a sofa in his office. He received a retainer from Hardwick every six months; not much but enough for him to agree to the business-man's terms. He could work on other cases but any time Hardwick needed his services he had to be available, without fail. The real money came from times like this. And whilst there was no denying the fact that Hardwick was a demanding taskmaster, he paid well.

Blake turned the facts over in his mind, jotting down the points in his notebook.

★　★　★

Facts:

At some point a headless corpse is inserted into the wrappings of a genuine Egyptian mummy.

The corpse and coffin are sold to

Lavelle — was the mixed-up corpse in place before the sale was arranged, or only after?

Lavelle cuts open the top of the mummy, exposing the stinking remains and creeping out those present. On examination the bandages have previously been sliced open underneath and the swap made that way.

Snell, the seller of the coffin, murdered a few weeks before the unwrapping.

Questions:

Who is the body?

Who murdered him and why? And why go to such lengths with the coffin?

Where are the rest of the mummy and the head of the corpse?

Why was Snell murdered — is it linked?

* * *

He sat back and propped his feet on the desk. Okay, he thought, could this just have been a weird way to get rid of a body? If someone, possibly Snell himself, had a body on his hands and was in possession of a handy coffin, there could be a temptation to put the two together. He could have cut off the head of the modern stiff — it would be easier to dispose of than a whole body and make it much harder to identify the corpse if it was discovered. But then, who killed Snell? A vengeful relative or friend of the dead man? It was possible. That would mean that the whole affair had nothing to do with Lavelle and his organisation.

Blake chewed the end of his pen. That hypothesis did not feel right to him. It was just too random. Looking down at his list of facts, he wondered about how long the corpse had been in place, like a cuckoo's egg waiting to hatch. Apparently Lavelle had received the coffin in October and had kept it in his study at Tanis Towers. Blake remembered how Lavelle had shuddered when he had realised that the corpse had been lying there decomposing all that time. It was a pretty gruesome thought, Blake had to admit. The coffin lid must have been very tightly sealed to have kept the stench in.

Moving on to another of his facts,

Blake wondered about the possibility of this having been done to get back at Lavelle and the Order — what was the name? He flipped back through his notebook. The Order of the True Sphinx. He shook his head in disbelief. To think that Hardwick, as tough and pragmatic a guy as he had ever known, bought into this rubbish. Still, one thing he had learned over the years was that people can always throw you a curveball.

He could call the Egypt Exploration Society and ask for their opinion of the Order, see if they showed as much animosity as Hardwick had towards them. There was also a bit of work to be done on checking out Lavelle himself. He had not been an Egyptian nut all his life, surely. There could be a jilted lover or envious rival in his past. Stomach rumbling with hunger pangs, he jotted down a note to himself to start that in the morning.

Five minutes later he was breathing in the greasy, salty, wonderful scent of the chip shop and devouring cod and chips washed down with tea. The takeaway did not have any tables, but he was allowed to go through to the back room to eat his food. The owner thought it was somehow glamorous to have a private investigator working upstairs and, on occasion, liked to hear about his work.

Replete with food and almost as full of questions, Blake said his goodnights to the chip shop owner and returned upstairs. A quick call to his police contact set his background checks in motion. He also got the number for the E.E.S. from the operator, noting that their headquarters were in London as he had guessed. Tomorrow, he would interrogate Jennings again and find out where Snell's circus was. If his intuition was anything to go on, the key to unravelling this knot would be there.

★   ★   ★

There was a loud rumble as Blake drove his car over the cattle grid. Before him, the track continued straight for about half a mile, becoming narrower by the yard so that the ragged brambles that grew on either side now threatened to rake at his vehicle. He changed gear and eased his foot off the accelerator, slowing the car right down so that he could negotiate the numerous potholes that pitted the uneven surface.

That there had to be an alternative route was definite, for how else could any of the circus folk get their much larger vehicles and trailers down here? Either that, or he was in the wrong place. He brought the car to a stop and reached for the map, which lay on the passenger seat along with the scribbled directions Jennings had hastily jotted down when he had visited him earlier that morning. He thought he had made the correct turnoff and that he was now on the right road. It was hard to be certain, what with these unclassified routes. Just another couple of hundred yards and he should reach Marsh End, the name given to the expanse of river meadow where he had learned Snell's circus folk had set up their temporary out-of-season encampment.

Unfastening his seatbelt, Blake got out, keeping his engine running, and took in his surroundings. Irrigation dykes filled with stagnant, smelly water separated the fields from the slightly raised levee now visible through a gap in the hedgerows over to his right. The agricultural fields on either side looked neglected, with only the occasional row of root vegetables emerging from the muddy ground and the tall, straggling weeds. Large black crows hopped about and some circled overhead, searching for carrion, their caws adding to the miserable, depressing scene. Crude scarecrows formed from rotting pumpkin heads and wooden cross-pieces lay here and there, inanimate guardians of a grey and largely forsaken land.

A sudden blare from a vehicle horn made him jump. Turning round, Blake could see a truck tearing down the track, coming towards him. Its approach was like a wild elephant trampling through the undergrowth, battering aside all in its path. And right now it showed no signs of stopping. The driver had to be blind or insane — or more likely stoned out of his head.

His heart thumping, Blake climbed

back in his car and threw it into first gear, pressing down on the accelerator. Tyres screaming in protest, he sped off, the looming shape of the oncoming truck a growing dark menace in the rear-view mirror. Wrestling with the steering wheel as the car bounced over a series of deep ruts, Blake worked through the gears, picking up speed. On either side, the bushes flashed past for thirty seconds or so, and then he was at a second cattle grid. He hit it at speed, feeling the rattling vibrations judder through his body as the steering wheel skidded from his hands. There was a wider bit of grass verge ahead. Stamping hard on the brake, he forced the car into a sharp right-hand turn, bringing it to a sudden stop.

Blaring its horn, the truck thundered past.

'Bastard!' snarled Blake. His knuckles whitened on the steering wheel as the anger raged within him. Out of the car windscreen, he could see that he had reached his destination — a vast open meadow which stretched for the best part of a mile before ending at a line of distant trees. To his right the grassland extended for a third of that distance before reaching the river, whilst to his left, beyond a barbed wire fence, he could discern more fallow fields. The track terminated some two hundred yards in front of him, where he could see an unsightly assortment of caravans, tents, trailers, parked cars and one or two motorbikes. The truck which had almost rammed into the back of him was now parking up outside one particularly decrepit-looking caravan.

Checking his watch, he saw that it was now ten minutes past two. Leaving the car where it was, he began walking towards the forlorn-looking, ramshackle encampment, his hands in his coat pockets. From past experience he knew that such a stance could instil wariness in others, for they could not be sure that he was not concealing a gun. And from the looks of this place, not to mention the unfriendly driver who had almost shunted him off the track, he would certainly have felt a lot more comfortable if he were armed.

The nearest caravan he was approaching looked a wreck; truly uninhabitable. The front door was missing and two of the windows had been smashed. The interior looked a mess — crammed furniture overturned and broken food cartons, crushed beer cans and empty cigarette packets lay all over the place, intermingled with the occasional dry dog turd. The exterior was just as bad, if not worse. Huge patches of mould and rust covered many of its surfaces, and its paintwork hung in strips like dead flesh from a leper.

Blake was about to proceed when an aggressive-sounding, deep-throated snarl prompted him to turn round. He found himself staring into the brown-grey eyes of a ferocious-looking Rottweiler, its black, gummy lips pulled back to reveal its huge fangs, its hackles bristling. It was slavering, as though in eagerness to rip him to shreds and feed on his mangled corpse.

'Who are you and what're you doing here?' called out a squeaky man's voice. There was an Eastern European twang to it.

Shuffling through the debris that lay inside the ruined caravan came a hideous dwarf with a warty, potato-shaped face. If ever Tolkien had wanted someone to play the part of something unpleasant from one of his books, then surely here was an ideal candidate. His hair was long and straggly and his front teeth were like those of a rat. He was dressed as a scruffy medieval court jester, the ripped patch-work garment of dull chequered colours, frilled cuffs and collar, and three-pointed cap complete with jingle bells giving him an even more creepy and sinister look. Black-and-red striped leggings covered his short legs. The costume was dirty and dusty, as though it had been stored in an old chest or an attic for a considerable time. On his feet he wore mud-encrusted boots. In one hand he held a marotte — a jester's stick — which was topped at the end with a head not unlike its owner's.

'Do you mind calling your dog back?' asked Blake. It was going to be hard enough talking to this man without having the threat of his shins being gnawed or his throat torn out hanging over him.

The diminutive jester removed a whistle from a pocket and gave it a soundless blow. Blake watched, relieved, as the Rottweiler immediately turned and slunk around the back of the caravan. He turned to its motley-wearing owner and gave a brusque nod. 'Thanks.'

'So what do you want?' There was a stark belligerence in the other's tone.

'I'd like to have a word with a Mr Horn,' answered Blake, using the name he had been given by Jennings. 'It's concerning the late Rupert Snell.'

The dwarf's look darkened, becoming a glower. There was something undeniably malign in his eyes as he stared fixedly at the private investigator before leaping down from the caravan. 'Mr Horn, you say?'

'Yes. Where can I find him?'

The dwarf's mouth twisted as he shrugged his shoulders.

'Is he here? If so, tell me!'

As though he had been suddenly struck both deaf and dumb, the ugly leprechaun-like being ignored the question and began picking his nose, burying his right index finger to the second knuckle. Blake had never had recourse to beat up a dwarf before but there could always be a first time. And as things were he would have liked nothing better than to teach this foul-faced munchkin some lessons in manners. He knew however that any physical attack on the other would in all likelihood bring a whole load of disreputables to his aid, not to mention the killer dog, and it would be he who would be on the receiving end of a beating. With this realisation in mind, he reached for his wallet and took out a five-pound note.

The dwarf's eyes lit up his grubby face. He removed his snotty digit. A grimy hand then reached out and snatched the money, making it vanish with a level of prestidigitation that took Blake by surprise.

'So where can I find Mr Horn?'

'Follow me.' With a peculiar waddling gait, the dwarf set off.

Blake followed. Now that he was entering the camp proper he could see more people. For the main they were a dark and mysterious-looking lot, and he doubted whether the bulk of them were British. The dwellings that they had set up were untidy and squalid and there was a noticeable makeshift look to everything. Even the vehicles were rust-buckets, and apart from the truck which he had encountered upon arrival he doubted whether any of them were roadworthy.

There was a cage in which a mangy black bear lay curled up inside. From somewhere nearby came the sounds of a heated argument and the barking of dogs. Aware now of the shifty-eyed looks that were being levelled at him, Blake proceeded with caution.

Standing at the entrance to a canvas tent on his right was a grossly fat, unsightly person who, due to the black bushy beard, he initially thought was a man. It was only upon noticing the huge breasts that he realised the other was in fact a woman. She threw him a mocking kiss and beckoned with a fleshy hand, inviting him to join her. No sooner had she done so than a tall and wiry man who had been seated on a chair nearby whittling at a piece of wood with a hand-axe got to his feet, a jealous look in his eyes. The right side of his wolfish, dirty and unshaven face was marked with a series of three deep, claw-like scratches, the central one of which extended from his jawline to his forehead, appearing either side of his right eye. His hair was long and spiked up with grease at the front. Like a prize hog, he sported a large gold ring through his nostrils.

This place was making Blake's teeth itch. The denizens of the Pit — the bare-knuckle fighting arena — had been threatening, but at least they were, relatively speaking, normal. Here, the people were both unusual and aggressive, almost to the point of open hostility.

The dwarf said something in his own language to which the man replied angrily. Then, grabbing Blake by the arm, he led him hurriedly away. 'I don't think Kagga likes you. He told me to tell you to stop making eyes at his wife. You'd better watch it. He can shave the hair off your head with his axes from fifty paces.'

'A pity he can't shave the beard off his wife's face,' Blake muttered. He was then steered towards a larger pavilion-type tent that had clearly seen better days.

The dwarf peered inside and said: 'Mr Horn. There's a man here to see you.'

A voice answered: 'Thank you, Zeb.' A moment later a tall, imposing man with dark hair and piercing green eyes stepped into the opening. There was a cold handsomeness to his face which was at complete odds with the rest of the grotesques who inhabited this place. He wore a black frock coat lined with blue silk and a crisp white shirt over expensively cut trousers. The effect was striking, as no doubt it was intended to be. He stared at Blake with the eyes of a skilled undertaker, taking in every detail as though sizing him up for his coffin. 'Yes, can I help you?' His words were spoken eloquently enough, although accented.

'I sincerely hope so. Can we speak inside?' Blake was feeling uncomfortable under the other's dark scrutiny. Of all the lawless and unpredictable people he had met in the course of his time as an undercover detective, there was something indefinable about this man that set the little alarm bells ringing inside his mind. He knew he would have to be careful. One false step and odds were he would not be leaving here without a struggle — one which he did not think he would win.

'By all means. Please.' Horn stepped aside and gestured for Blake to enter.

5

The interior of the tent came as a surprise to Blake. It was richly furnished with exotic cabinets, chairs, tables and chests. On the floor were several old and beautiful rugs covering the rough matting underneath.

Horn took a seat in the centre of the tent beside a small beaten-copper table. There was a tall metal coffeepot from which he poured himself a drink. He did not offer one to Blake. 'What is it that has brought you here? We don't have many visitors,' he said.

Blake calmly placed a chair opposite Horn's and sat down. He was not going to be left standing. 'I'd like to know all you can tell me about Rupert Snell.'

'And why do you want to know?' Horn asked, sounding almost bored.

'He sold something very unusual in the summer and it's caused a lot of trouble for my client. I'm an investigator.' Blake had decided on the drive there that he would not mention the corpse to begin with.

Horn sighed. 'I hope you're not looking for money. His estate's been wound up. All valid debts paid in full.'

'At the moment I just want information. What do you know about an ancient Egyptian sarcophagus that Snell apparently owned for many years? It's rather distinctive.'

Horn changed. It was subtle, but Blake recognised the signs. The man was now on edge.

'Oh, that old thing? Rupert had that as long as I knew him. He liked showing it to people — claimed it had been in his family for generations and was given to them by Giovanni Belzoni.' Horn curled his lip in a faint sneer. 'It made him feel important. He'd go on about the 'Great Belzoni' to anyone willing to listen. Belzoni was a circus strongman turned archaeologist, you see, and Rupert fancied himself as his natural successor.'

'It doesn't sound as if you liked him.'

'He was a difficult man; unreliable. If

he decided we would move on, even to another country, we all had to pack up — no discussions, no questions, no arguments.'

'Did he do that often?'

'Fairly. It made it very difficult for me to plan our performances. You see, I am the ringmaster but Rupert was the owner of the circus. When I joined the company it was touring Eastern Europe and was supposed to continue on to Turkey, but one night he suddenly told me we had to go back to England. His spirits had been talking to him.' Eyeing Blake suspiciously, Horn sipped a little more of his coffee.

'*Spirits?* Was he an alcoholic?'

'No! You misunderstand me. He was an occultist. He'd sit for hours trying to summon spirits or call up angels. Now I'll freely admit that we're not the most normal group of people, but even we thought it strange. He made most of his decisions according to all sorts of signs, omens and portents. The sarcophagus was only part of it. I was surprised when he said he'd sold it. I remember him saying it was very significant for his rituals.'

'*Rituals?* What kind of thing?' Blake was trying to get his mind round the very odd world Snell had inhabited.

'Like I said — raising sprits; asking for wisdom, power and guidance. All that kind of rubbish.' Horn talked off-handedly but Blake could tell this made him nervous. Perhaps he was not such a sceptic as he was making out. 'Even James got sick of it in the end and left.'

'James?'

'Rupert called him an acolyte, but slave would've been a better name. He thought he was going to learn all sorts of arcania, unlock the very secrets of the universe, but Rupert often had him filling in for crew who were ill or had left. Buying groceries and mucking out Bruno wasn't what James had in mind when he joined up.' Seeing Blake's look of confusion, he added with a condescending smile, 'Bruno's the bear.'

Blake was certain that Horn was feeding him a mixture of truth and lies. As most people did, in fact. It did not worry him. The more Horn talked, the more he would reveal, whether he liked it or not. 'Do you know the whereabouts of this James?' he asked.

'I'm afraid not. I don't even know his surname. He was Rupert's follower, not a performer. He up and left so suddenly I didn't know he'd gone until Rupert told me several days later.'

Blake felt the germ of an idea form. 'When did he leave?'

'Let's see. We'd just finished some shows in Middlesex, so that would've been sometime in mid-September.'

'And can you describe him?'

'Oh, pretty average. Mid-thirties, I'd say. Slim and a little short. Black hair swept to one side and a small Hitler-esque moustache,' Horn replied dismissively. 'No style whatsoever.'

Blake thought back to the body in the mummy wrappings. There was nothing to preclude James from being the unfortunate corpse, but nothing to rule him in either. It was certainly a possibility though. He decided to try a different tack. 'How did you find out that Snell had been murdered?'

Horn considered. 'It took about a week for the police to track us down. I'd taken the company to Warwickshire. Rupert didn't always come along with us and he'd decided to skip this time. I was extremely surprised at the news. When they first said he was dead I assumed it was self-inflicted. This was of course before they revealed the manner of his death. Most gruesome.'

'Suicide? That was your initial assumption?'

'Either that or accidental. He'd been very odd for a few weeks. Started accusing us of playing tricks on him, trying to spook him.' Horn laughed. 'Admittedly some of us have an unusual sense of humour, but he was just imagining things — disembodied heads, ghostly moans, that kind of thing. It was just after that, that Rupert left us to go home. I thought he was losing his grip. As I told you, he was deeply into the occult.'

'So when you heard he was, in fact, murdered, did you have any suspects in mind?'

'None in particular. Rupert was not the most honest of men, but I've known worse.' Horn stretched and stood up. 'Is there anything else? Because I do have work to get on with.'

Blake rose to his feet. He had plenty more questions, but there was more than one way to find answers. 'Thank you for your time, Mr Horn. It rather looks like my client will have to accept defeat and call in the police after all.' He was gratified to see a flash of fear in Horn's eyes.

'The police? Is that really necessary? You didn't say what was wrong with the sarcophagus that caused your client problems. Did it turn out to be fake?'

Blake walked to the edge of the tent. 'As far as I know, the casing was completely genuine.' He stepped out into the field, saying conversationally, 'The problem was its recently deceased occupant.'

'*What!?*' Horn gasped, his striking face looking much more ordinary without the sardonic smirk that had seemed to be a permanent fixture. 'You mean there was a real corpse in it, not just a mummy?' He certainly appeared to be shocked, but Blake could not be sure.

'Yes, at least except for the head. That was several thousand years old. The rest was completely modern — blue jeans, chequered shirt.' Blake was watching Horn closely.

'Christ! So that's what this is all about,' Horn exclaimed. 'The police will be all over us.' He grabbed a rickety wooden chair that was lying by the entrance to the tent, set it down on the grass and flopped onto it.

'I'm wondering if the body might be James. He fits with what little we could learn from the headless remains.' Blake looked with some satisfaction at the far less imposing figure Horn cut when he was troubled.

'You think Rupert *killed* him?' Horn thought for a few moments. 'Oh God, I suppose it's possible. They'd been arguing a lot and Rupert did have a temper.' His eyes widened. 'That would explain his weird behaviour — seeing phantoms, getting paranoid. It could all have been guilt. But then, who killed Rupert?'

'Did anyone ever come looking for James?'

'Not that I know of. They would have gone to Rupert's house anyway.'

'Perhaps they did,' Blake commented meaningfully. He was wondering how long he could keep the prospect of official intervention hanging over Horn. He knew that Hardwick did not want the police involved at all. As far as he was concerned, if Snell had bumped off someone, whether it was James or someone entirely unknown, and simply used the sarcophagus to get rid of the body, then there was no real connection between Lavelle and the corpse. That was all Hardwick really wanted to know. They could dump the remains and no one would be any the wiser.

He only had a few more questions for Horn. 'Was anyone from the circus involved in transporting the sarcophagus to its new owner?'

'Yes. I seem to recollect he got two of our roustabouts to do it. Look, do you really have to get the police in on this? I really don't think any of us would've been involved in disposing of a body, and Rupert himself is dead.' Horn looked up at Blake. 'It was bad enough when the police were investigating that, but they

100

cleared all of us from the enquiry. Some of my performers are what you could call . . . fragile. They could do without further interference.'

'Well . . . my real concern is to find out if the buyer of the sarcophagus and its contents was in some way targeted; but from what I can see, there's no sign of that, at least from the circus point of view. Did Snell have any family?'

'None that he ever mentioned. I think he was an only child and I do know his parents are dead. Certainly the only mourners at his funeral were his employees; and, myself aside, not that many of us bothered to go.'

Blake looked around at the dilapidated encampment. 'If Snell owned the circus, who does it belong to now?'

'Your guess is as good as mine! Some government official's supposedly working out if there are any heirs, for I doubt if they'll find a will.' Horn stood up, partially recovered from the shock of Blake's revelations. 'We're staying here over winter, then I think we'll go our separate ways.' The sardonic smile returned.

'Sometimes the show doesn't go on.'

'Well, thanks for the information. I can't promise not to inform the police of the corpse in the coffin. At the end of the day, it's not my decision to make. I can't, however, see much point in doing so.'

Ten minutes later Blake was back in his car, thankful to be leaving the place behind. He did not feel much further forward with the case, but with Snell dead there was a limit to what he could learn. Horn was a worry to him. He was sure that the man had been twisting the truth at times, but at others he had seemed genuine. One thing was certain: he was not about to start any strong-arm tactics in the middle of that rabble.

Blake would tell Hardwick what he had learned so far and let him decide the next move. He breathed a sigh of relief when he reached the main road. If he never had to see that place again he would be happy.

* * *

'The Order of the True Sphinx? Yes, I can tell you a bit about them. What in particular did you want to know?' The voice at the end of the telephone sounded slightly amused.

'What they do; how respected they are; who the key members are . . . that kind of thing. I'm writing an article called 'New Approaches to Ancient Facts'.' Blake had dreamed up the title on the drive back home as his cover story for contacting the E.E.S.

'Okay. Well, the Order champions most of the more outrageous interpretations of ancient Egyptian relics, writings and history. They put on lectures, publish papers and hold meetings to further their ideas. Regarding the members, there aren't that many — less than a hundred, certainly — and there's a kind of inner circle within that, centred around the founder member, Jeremy Lavelle.'

'So he's the one in charge?'

'Definitely. It's more of a personality cult than a society.'

'How is the Order thought of among the larger community of scholars of ancient Egypt?'

'Since you ask, the general consensus is

that it's a bunch of deluded idiots led by a charlatan.' The man laughed. 'We may of course be biased. Lavelle has one thing that we all covet — rich sponsors.'

'I can see how that might annoy people. So is the guy a complete fake? Just taking people for their cash?'

'To be fair, I think he believes quite a lot of his own hype these days, but that doesn't excuse his cock-eyed, half-baked theories based on the flimsiest evidence. There are quite a few people who are fascinated with the bizarre ideas that abound about the ancient Egyptians, and whether he's sincere or not, he's making money out of these 'pyramidiots', as we call them. I think he's just jumped on the Age of Aquarius, New Age, *Chariots of the Gods?* bandwagon.'

'Do you think there's a lot of ill-feeling towards Lavelle and the Order then?' Blake asked, thinking that perhaps there was malice at work here after all.

'If I'm honest, it's pretty obvious to any serious scholar that the Order's ideas are bunkum. The annoying thing is that Lavelle has hooked several big fish investors who would be very useful for the mainstream work that really needs doing in Egypt. Instead, they're putting money into attempting to prove that the Valley of the Kings was a rebuilding of temples found on Atlantis and the like. It's very galling.'

Blake spent a few more minutes blagging about other societies to give his story a ring of truth. Placing the receiver down, he considered what he had learned. The opinion that Lavelle was a fraudster fitted quite well with his own view of the man, and of course Hardwick must be one of the 'big fish'. He wondered if Hardwick actually bought all of the mumbo jumbo or in fact if he was in on some kind of scam. It was not stretching the bounds of credibility to imagine the latter. His police contact had turned up nothing of interest on Lavelle, not even parking fines, but there was quite a history on Snell. Mostly small-time stuff, but there had been an investigation a few years ago into suspicions that he used the circus as a convenient way to transport people with chequered pasts across borders without the proper authorisation.

Whatever the back story, Blake's brief was clear — discover how the corpse had got to Tanis Towers and, more importantly, why. He sighed. He was not doing very well on either front. Over the years he had found that the best way to keep clients from getting annoyed was to keep them up to date. A detailed report on avenues pursued sometimes helped to gloss over the lack of results. Accordingly, he called Hardwick and a meeting was arranged for the following day.

⋆ ⋆ ⋆

Lavelle sat back in the passenger seat and tried to calm his frazzled nerves. It was difficult. The past few hours had been ghastly. 'I'm really grateful for this,' he said to Braithwaite.

'Don't mention it,' Braithwaite replied. 'You sounded bad on the phone and like I said, we have the space. I'll let Don know so he can keep that investigator bloke in the loop.' He turned out of the gates of

Tanis Towers and headed out of town. 'I'm still a bit fuzzy on what's got you worried though.' He had telephoned Lavelle earlier to ask about a book he was hoping to borrow and found the man almost incoherent.

Lavelle took in a deep breath and let it out slowly, hoping to gather his thoughts before answering. 'It hasn't been a good day. This whole thing has been playing on my mind and the house still stinks. As it got dark, I thought I heard a sound coming from the study. I wish Don had taken the sarcophagus away as well as the body. Every time I see it I go cold.'

'I was surprised that he didn't. I know it's a bit bulky, but surely in that mansion he owns he could have found space.' Braithwaite sounded accusatory.

'Well, he said that I might want to hang on to it after all this is over. Frankly, I disagree. As I said, I heard a sound from the study. A whispering, hissing kind of sound. I thought maybe I'd left the phone off the hook or something and went in. There was nothing out of place that I could see, but it felt like I was being

107

watched. Then there was a crash from the kitchen and a scream.'

'*A scream?* Who was it?'

'No one. That's the problem. No one was there. No saucepans had fallen down or anything, but I know what I heard.'

'Could it have been an owl outside or something?' Braithwaite suggested.

'Possibly, but the next bit wasn't. I went to pour myself a drink and stood looking out of the kitchen window.' Lavelle paused and swallowed. 'I saw a head, just floating out there. Blood dripping from its neck.'

'You've got to be kidding!' Braithwaite swerved slightly as he glanced at Lavelle. 'You must've imagined it, Jeremy. That . . . that's just not possible. Either that, or you've been reading too many of my books.'

'Whatever the explanation, I'm damned glad not to be staying there tonight. Your call was like a lifeline to a drowning man.'

'You'll feel better soon. Henrietta has some food on and it'll do you good to be with other people. Only a little way to Adder Brook now. We should be there in twenty minutes. You had a terrible shock the other night. We all did. It's only natural it's had an effect on your nerves,' Braithwaite said placatingly.

For the moment Lavelle did not care. It was enough to be away from Tanis Towers.

6

To Blake's surprise, Hardwick telephoned him early in the morning and he was told to go to a new address some way out of town. He found the place on a map and worked out the route. It was a hamlet really, only four houses loosely strung out along a lane. He would hate to live so remotely himself, preferring the feeling of being right in the heart of things. It was good for his work and suited his way of life. Even when he had still been living at his flat, he never bothered to properly set up home. He liked to eat on the hoof and he knew all the fast food shop owners in his area. The pubs too were a good source of information, not to mention relaxation. He peered down again at the map. Adder Brook was at least five miles from the nearest village. He wondered again why Hardwick had chosen to meet him there.

When Blake finally found it, Adder Brook was just as remote as he had expected. The road to it was barely more than a track and all he could see were trees, fields and sheep. The last day of November was proving to be a cold one; the first time that winter he had needed to scrape ice off the car windscreen. The house he was looking for was number three — a fairly large and very old stone building which was almost as big as Tanis Towers. It was set in a garden of the kind that he could not stick — all neat rows and clipped topiary. Still, he had not come here to buy the place, just deliver a report. He knocked at the front door, noting the leering gargoyle knocker. Presently it was opened by a man he took a moment to place as being Braithwaite.

'Come in. We're all waiting for you,' Braithwaite said brusquely.

Blake bristled slightly, as he was actually on time, but followed the man inside. Entering the living room, he took a look at each person in turn, assessing their mood. Hardwick was slightly impatient, but controlled — no change there; Braithwaite eager; and Lavelle . . . The private investigator was shocked. Lavelle looked ill, with dark circles under his bloodshot eyes and a greyish cast to his skin.

'So, what've you got for us?' Hardwick got straight to it.

Blake began to relate his efforts and theories, such as they were, dwelling on minor details as he had little of real substance to report. He ended by saying that he had not discovered anything that pointed to a planned attack on Lavelle or the Order. He had been going to add that it may be worth visiting the circus again with a few heavies to see if anything else could be unearthed, but realised that Lavelle was shaking as if he had palsy. The other two had not noticed yet.

'What's wrong? Do you need a doctor?' Blake asked.

Lavelle started to laugh hysterically. Trying to get a grip on himself, he coughed and held tightly to the arm of his chair. 'Could you repeat what you said about Snell seeing and hearing things?'

'Horn reported that Snell claimed to be seeing phantoms a couple of weeks before his death; hearing ghoulish sounds, seeing floating heads . . . ' He broke off. Braithwaite and Hardwick were exchanging a meaningful look and Lavelle was slowly nodding. He had seen that sort of exaggerated control before, just before someone got hysterical. 'Can you tell me what's going on?'

There was a pause. None of them seemed eager to speak.

Then Hardwick gave Blake an annoyed look. 'I suppose you should know. Last night, Mr Lavelle believes he saw and heard something very similar to what you've described. That's why we've met here, in Mr Braithwaite's house. There's a possibility that Tanis Towers is . . . *haunted*.' He was obviously uncomfortable saying this, but his jaw jutted pugnaciously as if daring Blake to ridicule the possibility.

Blake had in fact been going to pour scorn on Snell's so-called phantoms. Reigning in his innate suspicion of anything supernatural, he tried to concentrate on Lavelle's very real reaction and the other two's sombre mood.

'I really don't feel good,' Lavelle muttered. 'I think I'm going to lie down for a while.' He left the room. Hardwick shut the door behind him and took out a packet of cigarettes. He lit up and breathed in.

'I don't really understand what's going on here,' Blake admitted. 'Do you want to fill me in?'

Hardwick sat down. 'Jeremy freaked out because if it's true that Snell was visited by phantoms in the same way he was last night, then might it not be that these things killed him? And if so, could they be gunning for Lavelle too?'

'But . . . surely you can't believe that?' Blake blustered. 'I mean, perhaps if the man had died of fright brought on by hallucinations I could concede a connection, but he died in a very real way. His bloody head was chopped off!'

'I once created a creature that got into the minds of its victims and made them beat themselves to death with a baseball bat,' Braithwaite commented with a certain amount of ghoulish glee, but he subsided at the look Hardwick gave him.

'Mr Braithwaite is a horror writer of some renown,' Hardwick explained with measured annoyance. 'Look, Blake. The fact remains that you still have no idea who the body is and why it turned up at Tanis Towers. Yes, you have theories, but not many facts. If, as you suspect, our headless stiff is this James character, there should be some trace of him somewhere. Horn probably knows more than he's letting on and you could do with taking another look at Snell's place, now that you've an idea what to look for. If James hung around with Snell for months there should be some trace of it.'

'Okay, I can do that. If I can at least get a surname for James that would help. I was wondering about Mr Lavelle's past. So far I haven't turned up anything that would warrant this kind of action being taken against him, but it would be helpful to have his input. I did ask for a list of anyone who might be considered an enemy but he hasn't given it to me yet. I'm not sure if this is the moment to ask him. Do either of you know of any possibilities?' Blake was aware that he might be about to venture into dangerous ground, but he had to ask the next question. 'My phone call to the E.E.S. suggested that at least some people believe the Order to be a somewhat fraudulent scheme. Have you had any trouble with disgruntled members?'

'Those *parasites*!' Braithwaite spat vehemently. He looked outraged. His fists clenched and he began to shake. 'They can't accept that we're driven by only the purest motives of scholarly and spiritual discovery.'

Hardwick, on the other hand, took the question seriously. 'I can't deny that we've had one or two people over the years who joined up, started paying the subscriptions and then changed their minds. I'll be the first to admit it's not for everyone. But anyone who wanted to leave could do so. I'm the treasurer and I just cancel their payments. No hard feelings.'

'Wait a minute! What about Thomas Surridge? He could well have had an axe to grind,' Braithwaite interjected excitedly.

'Who?' Hardwick asked with a frown.

'You know, the guy who looked like

116

Mephistopheles — goatee, widow's peak and all. He tried to muscle in on Jeremy a few years ago. Thought he should be the man in charge.'

'Oh, him.' Hardwick paused for a moment. 'Yeah, he was pretty strange, but I can't really see him as a murderer.'

'He did carry around a silver-bladed knife, you know,' Braithwaite pointed out.

'Jeez! I carry a gold lighter but it doesn't mean I'm going to set fire to you!' Hardwick protested. 'Although . . . it wouldn't hurt to at least find out what he's doing these days. I haven't heard anything of him since he stormed off. All right. Blake, I can find you the address he gave us when he joined. I think it's somewhere not far from here. You could do some sniffing around there.' Hardwick stood up and pulled on his camel coat. 'Charles, you'd better keep Jeremy here for a while. Staying at Tanis Towers would just freak him out until we get to the bottom of this. I mean, *we* know he didn't see anything supernatural last night, but just try telling *him* that. The sooner he gets back to normal the better. We can't have a nervous wreck leading the Order. Come on, Blake. Time to go.' So saying, he swept out of the house, the private investigator following in his wake.

Leaving the garden, Blake checked his watch. It was only half-past nine. 'Should I call your office to get the details for Thomas Surridge?' he asked Hardwick.

'Easier if you come to the office right now. Then you can get straight onto it. I'll see you there.'

Forty-five minutes later Blake emerged from Hardwick's glass-and-steel building with an address in the suburbs in his hand. Sitting in his car, he considered his next move. He did not particularly fancy a return visit to the circus right now. This Surridge character seemed rather less likely than Snell to be involved in the body switch, but it would in all likelihood be an easier interview. His mind made up, he started the engine and eased the car out into the traffic, heading for the suburbs and his meeting with 'Mephistopheles'.

★ ★ ★

Ringing the doorbell of a red-brick semi-detached house, Blake mentally recapped his cover story for this meeting. He had called Surridge from a telephone box, asking if he could have a chat about the Order of the True Sphinx for a piece of investigative journalism. Hopefully this angle would bring out any old grudges the man might hold, and if it did not — if Surridge was too complimentary about it, that itself could be concealing guilt.

The door was opened by a man who Blake would struggle to recognise as even slightly Mephistophelian. He was a little stout, clean-shaven, and although he did have that characteristic widow's peak hairline, his hair was neatly but not ostentatiously cut.

'Good morning. I'm Adam Blake. We talked earlier.'

'Oh, yes. Come in.' Surridge stepped back to allow Blake into the house. Taking him through to a small living room, he continued, 'I'm not sure exactly how I can help you, but I'm happy to talk about the Order and my experience of it.'

'Thank you. Firstly, how did you hear about them?'

'That would have been when I read an article by Jeremy Lavelle about the astrological symbolism of Old Kingdom pyramid layout and orientation. March 1968, I seem to recall. At the bottom of the page there was a piece about the author, and it mentioned the Order of the True Sphinx. I was intrigued, so I wrote to him. He got back to me and after a few letters back and forth I went to attend a meeting. It was fascinating. All sorts of people were there, and Jeremy gave a talk that fired me up.' Surridge smiled ruefully. 'He's a very charismatic speaker when he gets going, and we all felt swept up in his enthusiasm for the mysteries still to be revealed by the ancients.'

'So, was that when you joined as a fully paid-up member?' Blake asked.

'Yes, that very night. I sorted out the details with the treasurer and went home elated. Over the next two years I never missed a meeting or event. I think it's safe to say I was *obsessed*.'

'But not anymore? I believe you left the Order a couple of years ago?'

'Yes, in December 1970,' Surridge confirmed. 'As time went on I began to question things, do my own research. Jeremy didn't really encourage that. He'd lend people books from his own library and I came to realise that he never gave them anything that would contradict his own theories. I tried to have discussions with him, to talk about the new things I was reading, but he wasn't interested. After a while I got fed up. The Order could be so much more than Jeremy was letting it be, and most of the other members were content to get their knowledge from him. I realised that they weren't really that bothered whether the stuff he was feeding them was true or not. They just liked the ambiance and the thrill of feeling that they were discovering ancient secrets.' He shook his head. 'I was as bad as them to begin with but at least I started using my brain. When I finally got fed up, I tried to persuade people to leave the Order but they just didn't want to know. So in the end, I left. I'd wasted two years and quite a lot money and had nothing much to show for it.'

'What's your opinion of the people who run the Order?'

Surridge spent a minute considering. 'Lavelle's a self-important, blinkered egotist who knows just enough to sound good, but his theories are a load of rubbish. He has several people in a kind of inner circle who back him up. There's Sylvia Black. Quite a looker, if I remember rightly, but too intense for me. Larry Williams; he's got a job at a university and I would say he gets a kick out of doing something the academics wouldn't approve of. Charles Braithwaite; he writes quite good horror stories and buys the ancient Egyptian stuff hook, line and sinker. And Don Hardwick. Of all of them, he's the one who could stand up to Jeremy when he wanted to. He was, and I assume still is, the treasurer and never had trouble getting money out of people. Don't get me wrong, I'm not accusing him of anything. I just mean that you tended not to forget to pay up on time after you'd been reminded by him. I often wondered how he got into the Order in the first place. Of all of them, he didn't really seem the type.' He looked at Blake questioningly. 'If you're investigating the Order for an article, has something happened to prompt this? A claim of fraud, for example?'

'You sound like that wouldn't surprise you,' Blake answered evasively. He had to be careful not to start a rumour that might somehow get back to Hardwick.

'Well, it would be easy to fleece some of the people who are in the Order. Original thought isn't exactly encouraged.' Surridge's eyes suddenly opened a bit wider as he remembered something. 'Actually, just before I left I did hear something about wills that got me thinking. It was Hardwick's idea, I think, to invite members to consider including a donation to the Order in their will — some kind of financial covenant. I can imagine that going down like a lead balloon with some of the relatives. Did you know about that?'

'No. I'm mostly going on what I've heard about Lavelle from a different source, which I can't divulge yet. You've been most helpful, Mr Surridge. It'll take me some time to finish my article, but I'll be sure to send you a copy.' Blake got ready to leave but wanted to ask one more question. 'How much would you say you regret getting involved with the Order?'

Surridge chuckled. 'Not hugely. It was a mid-life crisis kind of thing and was probably less damaging than buying a sports car or running off with the neighbour's wife. It's just a rather silly society that has ideas well above its station. There's nothing really sinister or cultish about it. When I look back on it the whole thing feels rather pathetic. Not much there for an exposé, I'm afraid.'

And not much motive for sending a body to Lavelle, Blake thought as he made his goodbyes. He was inclined to take Surridge at face value. He had not seemed nervous or over-confident or done any of the tell-tale things that Blake recognised as hiding a guilty conscience. He could of course just be a very good actor — psychopaths often were — but there seemed no reason to investigate him further at this point. Surridge's views about the inner circle were interesting but hardly illuminating. He already knew that Hardwick was a tough nut and had decided Braithwaite was just a nut. Sylvia Black and Larry Williams were unknown quantities he had yet to meet. He sighed. There was nothing else for it. He would have to go back to Snell's house and then go and see Horn and his charming collection of misfits.

* * *

Blake was approaching Snell's abandoned barn when, through his car windscreen, he saw a small plume of greyish-black smoke spiralling into the wintry sky. Bringing his car to a stop, he parked up on the side of the lane, unfastened his seatbelt, reached for his jacket which lay on the passenger seat, and got out.

A chill wind gusted between the tall hedgerows on either side, carrying with it the smell of burning wood and leaves. Zipping up his jacket, Blake quietly locked his car. He stood for a moment, thinking things through. It was possible that Jennings had lit the fire, but it seemed highly unlikely, as surely the last thing he wanted was to call attention to his presence. No, there had to be something else behind this. Slowly he crept forward, hoping that whoever was doing the burning had not heard his approach.

Around the outskirts of the property, on the side he was approaching from, was a ragged, ten-foot-high laurel hedge. Using this as cover, Blake peered through into the extensive back garden. He could see a man he was certain was not Jennings, his back to him, stoking a small bonfire. Beside him there was a pile of boxes and he was unceremoniously reaching inside, removing papers and magazines and throwing them onto the fire. It did not take a genius to reach the conclusion that he was up to no good — destroying evidence from the looks of it. Either that, or he was searching for something and was disposing of anything considered superfluous.

There was a gap in the hedges to Blake's left. He was in a dilemma. He knew that the longer he deliberated, his inaction risked a greater chance of losing vital information. Yet to challenge the unknown individual, unarmed as he was, posed its own problems. Matters were made worse when, seconds later, he saw a large Rottweiler come padding out from the rear of the barn. It was then that the man moved to one side and he saw his face.

It was Kagga, the scarred, nose-ringed character from the circus! And the dog undoubtedly belonged to Zeb, the ugly dwarf.

This was confirmed seconds later when the midget staggered out from the doorway, laden with two large leather bags filled with books. Bizarrely, he was still dressed in his scruffy motley. Cursing, he waddled to the bonfire and dumped them down. He said something to his scrawny accomplice in his own language and then, accompanied by his ferocious dog, he returned inside.

Blake knew he had to do something but his options were limited. There was no denying the fact that the longer he delayed the more potential evidence would be destroyed. Yet he was not all that keen on the idea of tackling these two nefarious characters as well as the dog. Had he a gun things would have been different.

He was wracking his brains for a solution. He could find a telephone box and call the police, informing them that there were arsonists setting fire to the place, but that would take too long; and anyway, it contradicted Hardwick's wishes.

Having now emptied the two leather holdalls, Kagga looked appraisingly at them, clearly wondering whether they were worth keeping before coming to a decision and throwing them on the fire.

The hideous gnome shouted something from inside the house. Kagga spat. He cursed savagely and stomped inside.

Potentially vital incriminating evidence was going up in smoke before Blake's very eyes and although he had been unable to uncover anything on his first search, he was certain that there was something of importance still to be found. Otherwise, why were these two disreputables going to such lengths to destroy it? In just what way were they involved? Had they been sent here by Horn?

From the sound of it the two were at loggerheads, engaged in a heated argument. Stealthily Blake sneaked out. His nerves were afire as adrenaline surged through his body, preparing him for the fight or the flight which was no doubt imminent. Resting atop a rusty garden ornament which had once served as a plant holder, he could see a hand-axe, probably Kagga's. He picked it up and then slinked around the far side of the barn. He had just reached the corner when he heard the two of them come out. They were cursing and bickering, both clearly unhappy with each other's company and with the task which they had been allocated.

Knowing that he risked being sniffed out by the dog, Blake continued around the front of the barn. Reaching the main door, he gently pushed it open and peered inside. Much of it was as he remembered it — a complete mess. There were piles of circus flyers strewn over the floor close to the remains of Jennings's camping gear. It was only then that his thoughts turned to the squatter. Where the hell was he? Had he taken his advice and got out, or had he fallen foul of the dwarf and his bearded-lady-loving side-kick?

Unsure as to exactly what it was he planned on doing, Blake edged cautiously inside. He knew there would be no reasoning with these two unsavouries if he were to be caught snooping around. It was just possible that he might be able to snatch some piece of valuable evidence before it was consigned to the flames. Closing the door behind him, he stood for a moment listening to the sounds of the house and the voices of the two men outside. Steeling his courage, he sneaked to his right, entering the kitchen.

There was an uncomfortable prickling along his spine and with every step he took he had the sensation that he was being watched. Perspiration formed on his forehead and he wiped it off with a shaking left hand, the knuckles of his right hand white around the haft of the hand-axe. He was about to cross over to the passage which led to the bedrooms when a sudden snarl rose beside him and a blur of black fur leapt through the air. With a cry he pulled back, and then the dog was attacking him, tearing at his arm. The pain was excruciating.

Blake brought the chopper down, striking the beast a glancing blow which severed one of its ears. Still it hung on, its fangs digging deeper through his now-bloodied jacket sleeve.

Repeatedly, Blake hacked at it. He was a dog lover himself but he knew his very survival was at stake. If this creature were to bring him down it would tear out his throat and rip him to pieces. For that reason he let out one final, savage cry and, chopping deep into the Rottweiler's head, he killed it.

The hefty animal had no sooner slumped to the linoleum in a pool of blood, the sharp-bladed weapon embedded in its skull, than the back door opened. The bizarrely dressed dwarf fixed Blake with a look of utter hatred. His face was now a hideous, gargoyle-like mask of pure rage and, screaming like a maniac and pulling a knife from his belt, Zeb came running towards him.

The dwarf was not at ideal punching height but he was damn well kickable. Leaping up to one side, Blake did exactly that, striking out with a right foot which landed hard and firm on the small man's chest. The force of the blow sent him reeling and knocked the knife spiralling from his hand. He moved in quickly and, grabbing the evil jester by the outrageous costume he wore, he lifted him and threw him to one side.

Suddenly, from behind, a pair of dirty hands clenched around his throat, ragged nails puncturing the skin. Reaching back, Blake grabbed a handful of greasy hair and pulled savagely. His attacker cursed and released his hold, just in time for a bunched fist to strike him full in the face.

Uttering a curse, Kagga staggered back, blood leaking from his busted nose. He then went forward, arms flailing, head down, pummelling into Blake. Together they crashed back, collided with a chair and fell to the floor.

Scrambling to his feet, Blake grabbed

the other by his dirty shirt and was just about to smash his right fist into the nose-ringed, angular face when Kagga jabbed him in the stomach. All the wind seemed to rush out of his lungs. A follow-up uppercut sent him staggering back, his head temporarily swimming. Kagga shouted something unpleasant-sounding.

Wiping blood from his lips with the back of his hand, Blake then rushed at his attacker. Kagga pulled back so that they were now both in the main room once more. He met the private investigator's charge with a swing from a bunched fist, all of his wiry muscle behind the punch.

Blake had anticipated that this would be coming, and this instinct made him double up swiftly so that the jab smote into his side and not into the pit of his already pummelled stomach. The blow still sent a stab of agony lancing through him and he fell back, narrowly avoiding Kagga's next swing. To his dismay, he could see that although clearly injured, Zeb was getting back to his feet.

There was a mad, almost berserk look

in Kagga's eyes as he lashed out with a fist which caught Blake just below the left eye. Lights flashed in front of him as he fell back, stumbling to the floor. Then, screeching like a wild cat, Kagga threw himself forward, boots first.

Desperately, Blake twisted his body, getting himself out of the way of those booted heels that came streaking for his throat. There was no mistaking his attacker's intentions now — he meant to kill.

Kagga landed awkwardly as the jar of the impact shuddered through his legs and up into his body. He let out a bellow, a huge shout compounded of pain and rage. By the time he had regained his balance, Blake was back on his feet.

With a deft move, Blake sprang behind the long-haired circus character and drove in two quick kidney punches. Then, grabbing him in a headlock, he applied all of his strength, hoping to squeeze the life from the other or break his neck. His grip tightened as the man squirmed in a frantic effort to free himself.

The front door slammed shut. Like

some bogeyman from a child's nightmare, Zeb emerged from the shadows, his knife gleaming in the poor light.

Blake threw Kagga to the floor and backed away. Coming quickly to the conclusion that whatever vital clues these two were trying to destroy were not worth risking his life for, he made a run for it. The wounds from the dog bite and the brawl he had just been in sent jolts of pain stabbing through his body. Heading for the back of the house, he brushed aside a beaded curtain and rushed out into a short corridor. Two doors, one leading to the bathroom, the other a small bedroom, were on his right whilst straight ahead there was another door leading to an extension. Pursued by angry shouts and his unevenly sized attackers, he ran along the passage and threw open this door.

There were two steps down into the space beyond which was filled to the ceiling with a wide array of junk — spare car parts, crates, boxes and rusty garden implements. The door directly in front was panelled with a square of opaque glass, permitting him to see that it led outside. The wooden floor creaked ominously as he ran over to it, his heart sinking when he discovered the door securely locked. It was then that, amidst the clutter, he saw an upright sarcophagus, its lid slightly ajar. There was a darkened space beyond that appeared far bigger than it should have been — some kind of secret room!

Jabbering like a lunatic, Zeb stumbled along the corridor. From some distance behind him could be heard Kagga's snarls.

Suddenly the hand-axe with the dead dog's brains still dripping from the blade thudded into the coffin lid inches from Blake's head. Knowing that there was no other means of escape, Blake sucked in his stomach and went, shoulder first, into the sarcophagus. He had only taken two short steps when the ground disappeared from beneath his feet and he was falling. Crashing down a flight of rickety wooden steps into the dark, he landed painfully on the ground. Dazed, he looked over his shoulder.

Zeb was at the top of the stairs. In one hand he held the door of the sarcophagus. In the other, he gripped a can of petrol. Giggling sadistically, he began pouring the flammable liquid down the steps.

Such was his pain that Blake could only watch in stunned horror as the dwarf struck a match and sent a line of liquid fire streaking down the stairs towards where he lay. The sarcophagus lid was then slammed shut.

7

Panic seized Blake. Overcoming his pain, he got quickly to his feet, backing away from the flaming stream. A puddle of fire had formed at the bottom of the steps and to his horror he saw there were several other petrol cans less than a couple of feet away. Knowing full well that if they were to combust the whole basement would be transformed into an incinerator, he limped over and hastily carried them away from the fire's reach.

The heat that now emanated from the burning stairs was ferocious and he knew that escape that way was impossible. The treads began to warp and char, black patches spreading like a voracious mould. A thick, choking dark smoke filled the low ceiling.

Eyes stinging, he looked frantically around for something of use, anything which would enable him to extinguish the fire. His hopes rose upon seeing a large sheet of thick tarpaulin that had been thrown in a corner. Dragging it clear, Blake's heart lurched in his chest. Hidden beneath, his corpse displaying numerous deep cuts undoubtedly caused by blows from a hand-axe, was Jennings's decapitated body. His severed head lay nearby, the blood-filled eyes staring sightlessly at the ceiling.

Fighting back an urge to vomit, Blake managed to steady himself. A fresh wave of anger surged through him. Grabbing the heavy sheet of tarpaulin, he threw it over the flaming oil patch and began stamping on it. The heat from the burning stairway was fierce but in his rage he hardly felt it. Lifting the dense covering, he hefted it over the steps. With alarm, he noticed that his right trouser leg was burning and he beat at it with his hand. It was painful but he succeeded in putting it out.

Then, with a crash, the stairway collapsed.

Blake leapt back. While the fire had been raging he had noticed where the light switch was. Now that the blaze was more or less out and things were getting dark, he went over and flicked it on.

Light from a bare bulb hanging from the ceiling lit up the secret basement.

Picking up a corner of the smouldering tarpaulin, Blake dragged it across the floor and covered the dead body, glad not to have to look at it again. He could hear nothing from those bastards who had tried to roast him alive down here and he clung to the hope that they believed him dead. Looking at the wrecked stairway, he could tell that escaping from this place was not going to be easy. The back of the sarcophagus lid — the secret door — was a good ten feet above him; and what was more, it had undoubtedly been locked.

Now that the immediate threat had been taken care of, Blake turned his attention to the room. It was clear that Zeb and Kagga had been down here — evidence of their rummaging was clearly visible to his trained eye.

After several minutes spent searching, he was about to give up on finding anything of significance and instead focus his attention on getting out, when he

140

spotted a small door cunningly concealed behind an empty bookcase. Intrigued, he investigated it further and was surprised to find that the bookcase shifted readily to one side. The door had neither a handle nor a lock, yet it opened easily enough when he pushed it.

The room beyond was no bigger than the one he had just come from. Its interior was shadowy and he had to stoop in order to get inside. Light from the main basement enabled him to discern something of its furnishings; and what he saw took him by surprise, for it appeared that the room was some kind of shrine. It reminded him of Lavelle's study in the way it had been designed to resemble an ancient Egyptian tomb. Occult symbols had been crudely painted on the walls, and there was a small altar in the far corner.

Edging inside, Blake could see several items on the offering table: two web-covered candlesticks; a thick, dusty leather-bound book; an Egyptian statuette of a black-skinned pharaoh; a chalice; and a wavy-bladed dagger.

It was time for Blake to take a reality check. This was like something from a

Dennis Wheatley novel or a Hammer horror film. All that it was missing was for Christopher Lee to come groaning and lumbering out of the shadows swathed in filthy bandages. Psychopathic killer dwarfs, headless corpses, and now this. If he managed to get out of here, he would be having strong words with Hardwick about a pay increase. Additionally, access to a gun was becoming a pressing concern.

With a growing sense of unease, he approached the shrine. The fact that there was dust on the book and spider webs on the candlesticks strongly suggested to him that this strange sanctuary had not been used for some time. Several months at least — which tallied in well with the date of Snell's murder. That the man had been involved in the black arts or something as equally diabolical was now evident. Horn had told him as much, but to see the proof with his own eyes . . .

A shudder went through Blake as he picked up the book. Pentacles and ancient Egyptian hieroglyphs decorated the frontispiece. He knew that whatever was contained within its yellowed pages was beyond him.

He flicked briefly through it and a piece of paper fell out. He bent to pick it up and was shocked to see a photograph of Lavelle. It looked like it had been cut from a magazine, but there was a strange design drawn over the man's face in black ink. He could not think of any sensible reason why Snell would have this, hidden away down here, if there were not a suspicious motive behind it. He tucked it back into the book and turned his attention to the statuette. He had seen several things like this amongst Lavelle's collection, although this one was peculiar due to its ebony-black skin. He knew next to nothing about ancient Egyptian statuary but it looked to him like a pharaoh.

There was nothing else of interest in the room and he took one last look before ducking back into the basement. He looked at his wristwatch, gauging that he would wait down here for another hour before making his escape bid, hopefully by which time Zeb and Kagga would have cleared off. The bookcase looked sturdy enough to take his weight, and if he were to prop it against the wall where the destroyed stairs were, he figured he could use it as a makeshift ladder, enabling him to reach the lintel above. Then it would be a case of pulling himself up and battering the door down.

He sat in a corner and looked through the book. He reckoned it to be a couple of hundred years old. There was a dry rustle from its pages as he leafed through it. There were diagrams and sketches and weird passages written in obscure languages, none of which made any sense to him.

His hour of waiting up, Blake hatched his escape plan. It proved successful as far as getting up to the door, but opening it was another matter entirely. He managed to push it open an inch or two, but his would-be killers had blocked it with something. His problem was compounded due to the restricted space in which he found himself, balanced somewhat precariously on the narrowest of ledges, the book clamped under one arm. Bracing himself in the doorway, he managed to get into a position whereby he could push out with his feet. In this manner, he forced the opening wider. Gritting his teeth, his veins cording in his neck, he exerted all of his strength and suddenly something gave. There was a loud crash on the other side and he overbalanced, almost falling back into the basement. Madly he reached for the door jambs and, breathing heavily, hauled himself out of the upright sarcophagus.

Blake spent a minute catching his breath and regaining his composure. At least there was no sign of the 'gruesome twosome'. Making his way stealthily through the house, he sneaked out the back door.

The bonfire was still smoking. Most of whatever had been thrown on it was now a heap of smouldering ash. Noticing a black ledger, he bent down and removed it from the fire. The pages had curled and most were blackened, but a partially burned black-and-white photograph drew his attention. Wiping away the soot and the ash, he put it in his pocket. He was about to turn away when a bit of tanned leather caught his eye. Raking the item out with a stick, he saw it was a wallet — quite badly burned on the outside, but the leather might have protected the contents. He pocketed it and decided to inspect his finds from the safety of his car.

* * *

Blake sat in his car for a long time, ready to speed off at the first sign of trouble. His body hurt almost everywhere and his heart continued to race. This encounter was the closest he had ever been to death and it was taking its toll. He investigated the dog bite, easing the material of his jacket and shirt aside to assess the damage. It was not too deep, but he reckoned it should be looked at by a doctor. The last thing he wanted was an infected wound. Still, he finally had several things of importance to report to Hardwick and the others.

Looking at his finds, Blake opened the wallet first. As he had hoped, the interior was relatively intact; and although there was no money inside, there was a driver's license. The small passport-sized photograph showed a man with a short, square moustache just as Horn had described, and sure enough the license belonged to a Mr James Ryan, thirty-three years old. Examining the singed fragment of the photograph he had plucked from the bonfire, he saw five figures dressed in weird robes. Infuriatingly, the face of the individual on the far right was burnt away. The one next to it was Snell, his face familiar to him from the countless circus flyers he had found strewn about the place. The man standing beside him was Ryan. So this was Snell's former acolyte and, if his suspicion were correct, the man whose headless corpse had been palmed off on Lavelle. The figure on the right was in all likelihood a woman, but due to the mask she wore it was impossible to ascertain her identity. In front of her was a semi-naked diminutive figure which again, although masked, was surely Zeb. From the background details Blake could see that the photograph had been taken in the main large room of Snell's house, which had been made to look more exotic with low lighting.

Deciding that his first port of call would be Hardwick's office, Blake started the engine and carefully put the car into gear, his left arm throbbing with pain. Grimacing as he released the handbrake, he pulled away.

He revised his plan as he approached the city. If he turned up at Hardwick's office looking like this, his employer would not be pleased. As he was hoping to negotiate extra danger money, it would not be sensible to antagonise him. Accordingly, he pulled into the car park of a pub not far from the centre and got him on the telephone. He had just had time for a pint and a packet of peanuts when Hardwick arrived, looking uncharacteristically tense.

'What the hell happened to you?' Hardwick exclaimed, taking in the cuts and bruises and the torn, bloody left arm of Blake's jacket. 'You smell like a burnt sausage.'

'Attacked by a dog and two murderous lunatics. Then I was nearly incinerated and buried along with the pharaohs,'

Blake said calmly. He took a sip from his pint. 'There was also another decapitated corpse. Jennings — remember I mentioned him? I think his death was a case of wrong place at the wrong time. Poor bastard!'

'So I take it we're finally getting somewhere.'

'I certainly hope so. I'd hate to think they just didn't like my face.' Blake had not expected sympathy from Hardwick so he was not surprised at his pragmatic approach. 'I'll need to get this cleaned up but I wanted to fill you in first. I saw Surridge this morning and I think we can rule him out, particularly in the light of this new evidence. Then I went up to Snell's place and saw two of the people from the circus burning papers from the house. They objected to my interference and did their level best to kill me.'

'What did you find out? Do you know who's behind all of this?'

Blake reached into a pocket and brought out the photographs and the black pharaoh figurine. 'Look familiar?'

'That's Lavelle!' Hardwick exclaimed,

taking the smaller of the two photographs. 'It's the picture he uses for magazines. Someone's drawn an inverted ankh over it.'

'Does that mean something?'

'Yes . . . it's the sign of death and eternal damnation. Where the hell did you find this?'

'I found it in a creepy shrine hidden beneath the house. This one — ' Blake handed over the fire-damaged photograph. ' — shows Snell. He's the one in the ornate headdress. I know it's him because there were a few photos of him in the house; promotional shots for the circus. The smaller man to the left of him is James Ryan; and as I found his charred wallet in the bonfire, I think we can work on the assumption that it was his decapitated body in the sarcophagus. I'll check with the police for his details, but I believe we'll find he hasn't been in touch with anyone since the summer. So what do you make of this photograph?'

Hardwick stared at it for a long moment then let out his breath. 'I don't like the look of this. You say this is Snell?

Well he's wearing the robes of an ancient Egyptian high priest. Ryan's just a follower, but the midget is dressed up as Bes. He was a kind of protector god who drove away evil.'

'Ha! The only protection that character would be involved with is the Mafia type.'

'There's a difference here,' Hardwick continued, ignoring Blake. 'Something's wrong about the set-up but I can't put my finger on it. It's like this statue. It's ringing a bell somewhere.'

'The whole thing is bizarre as far as I'm concerned, and I've saved the oddest thing for last.' So saying, Blake took the grimoire out from the seat beside him and put it down on the table.

Hardwick's eyes widened. He gingerly picked it up. 'Was this in the shrine as well?' he asked quietly.

'In pride of place,' Blake confirmed. 'Do you know what it is?'

Hardwick opened the book and flicked through some of its age-worn pages. 'In a manner of speaking. I don't know hieroglyphics, not properly, but I can recognise a few things. More to the point,

I've seen something like this before, with the symbols and patterns. It's a book of rituals, spells if you like. This must have been the stuff that Snell and his cronies got up to.'

'Do people actually do this kind of thing for real?' Blake asked curiously.

'Some do, yes. There was quite a craze for magic about forty years ago and various individuals and groups, such as the Ordo Templi Orientis and the Hermetic Order of the Golden Dawn, dedicated huge amounts of time trying to replicate the ancient rituals that we know the ancient Egyptians practised.'

'Surely that's just superstitious nonsense? Magic doesn't really work.' Blake could not help scoffing at the thought.

Hardwick regarded him coldly. 'So you know all there is to know about the universe, do you? Let me tell you, there is a lot more to this kind of thing than you realise. I've been to Egypt, many times. I've chanted at the foot of the Sphinx as the sun rose on the Giza plateau. This is not just nonsense.'

Blake tried to hide his surprise. The

image of Hardwick wearing a kaftan and singing to the sun was preposterous. The man had made his fortune selling heavy plant machinery, for God's sake!

'Magic was a way to ask for help from the gods; to exert control over the weather, to assist people. The vast majority of it was intended to be beneficial.' Hardwick put his hand on the grimoire. 'This, however, strikes me as being the other side of the coin.'

'You mean that there's bad stuff; raising demons or something?'

'Not demons, but asking for your enemies to be struck down, for example.' Hardwick was ruffled. 'I'm going to have to find out more about this. I'd ask Jeremy, but there's no way I'd show this to him if he's the intended target. It could push him completely over the edge.'

'Do you mean this is like voodoo or something?' Blake asked incredulously.

'It might be. The corrupted mummy and corpse could be like a psychic poison and by unwrapping it, Lavelle got contaminated. We need someone who knows about these things.'

'Well, is there anyone else in the Order who could help?'

'Our most knowledgeable member was Professor Steven Douglas, a retired Egyptologist who had worked on the Abu Simbel project when they raised the Aswan High Dam. Unfortunately he died a few years ago. With Douglas gone and Jeremy unavailable, the best we've got remaining is Braithwaite.' Seeing Blake's expression, he added, 'You'd be surprised how much he knows. He's been part of the inner circle for over ten years and is passionate about the Order's interests. I don't want news of this book to get to Jeremy. I'll call Charles and get him to meet us away from the house.'

'Do you want me to do anything about Jennings; report his death to the police?'

'No.' Hardwick was definite. 'It'll just complicate things. He'll be discovered sometime, unless the dwarf and the other guy move him. We've more important things to do.' He gazed around the pub. 'This is too public a place for my liking. I've got a few things I need to put in motion. You go and get that arm seen to.

I'll call you at seven o'clock.'

Blake checked his watch. That gave him a few hours to see a doctor, wash and get something to eat. 'Okay. I'll be by the phone at seven.'

'Make sure you are.' Hardwick gathered up the book, the photographs and the statuette. 'You might want to open your mind a little, Blake. Cynicism is a sensible starting point but it's not that different from ignorance, and ignorance can kill.' Leaving the private investigator to ponder this, he left.

★　★　★

Back at his office — washed, dressed and with his wound cleaned and bandaged — Blake was self-medicating with his favourite meal from the Diamond House Chinese takeaway. The physical and mental strains of the day were catching up on him and, coupled with the food, he was in danger of falling asleep. Realising he was beginning to nod, he walked to the window and opened it, letting the cold night air in.

He thought back over the attack. Where were Zeb and Kagga now? Would they just assume that he was dead, or would they go back to check? Without knowing more about them or who, if anyone, they were working for, he could not make much of an informed guess. Horn seemed a likely culprit.

He had called up his police contact again; he was racking up a whole heap of favours there, and a preliminary look through the system had not turned up anything of note for James Ryan — no record, no missing persons report. He had the man's address and it would be worth checking out.

Blake stopped, a spicy chicken wing halfway to his mouth. What if Ryan was the murderer? The body in the coffin could be a complete unknown, some tramp even. Ryan could have killed Snell, perhaps with help from Zeb and Kagga, and set the whole thing up to get at Lavelle. It was possible. Hell, anything was possible with this weird case. If he were to dig deep enough he was certain he would find that everyone had a motive.

Everybody was a potential suspect; the problem was, there were too many of them.

It would be helpful if he could show Lavelle the driver's license on the off-chance that he might recognise Ryan. It was frustrating that Hardwick and Braithwaite were so protective of the man. He could understand that Lavelle could be in physical danger, but they seemed far more worried about his mental state — obsessed with maintaining him as the figurehead of the Order. Why was this? Was it just due to bonds of friendship, or was he truly irreplaceable? Was there something they had not told him? He would have to ask Hardwick about it.

The phone rang. 'Yes?' Blake answered immediately.

'Hardwick here. We're going to meet at Tanis Towers in an hour's time. Got that?'

'Yes.'

The phone went dead.

Blake finished his food and went into the back room. Reaching under the sofa, he dragged out a large metal box about a foot deep and a foot and a half long. Unlocking it, he rummaged inside. He took out his camera; he wanted to take some shots of Tanis Towers and he had been lazy about carrying it around lately. There was also a blackjack which found its way into his pocket. He had decided against getting a gun. He knew from past experience that there were too many things that could go wrong with a firearm in one's possession.

It would not take him that long to get to the house — about forty minutes — but he wanted to get there ahead of the others if possible and have a scout around the gardens.

The traffic was light and he was the first there. The house was all in darkness and he took the torch out of his glove compartment. Apart from the gravel drive, the area to the front of the house was a wide lawn, with no places for anyone to hide. Moving round the house to the left, the lawn continued and was joined by small trees — probably apple trees, but it was hard to tell — and areas of planting. At the back of the garden

158

there were some taller trees and a thick hedge. All seemed to be quiet.

He looked up at the house with its two turrets sticking up like horns. He wondered if running the Order had paid for all of this. If so, someone could easily want to muscle in on Lavelle's cushy set-up. The more he thought about it, the more convinced he became that Lavelle and not the Order was the intended target.

There was a crunch of wheels on gravel and a beam of light spilled round the edge of the house. Blake walked back to the front door and saw Braithwaite getting out of his car. The horror writer was wrapped up against the cold.

'Hardwick not here yet then?' Braithwaite asked.

'No, but it's only seven-fifty. He shouldn't be long.'

'I understand that you've made some important discoveries today?'

'Yes. I'll go through it all when we're inside, but I think we're getting close now. Close enough that I'm lucky to be alive.'

Braithwaite's eyebrows shot up. 'What happened? Was it Thomas Surridge?'

'Did Hardwick tell you anything about it?' Blake asked.

'Not a lot. Just told me to get over here and not to mention it to Jeremy. Ah, here he is now.'

Hardwick's car pulled to a stop and the American got out. He was carrying a holdall and the keys to the house. 'We'll talk inside, gentlemen,' he said, unlocking the door and switching on the lights.

They got settled in the living room, which was a little chilly. Blake spotted radiators but guessed it was such a big house that in winter the log fires were a necessity. Indeed, before shedding his bulky coat, Braithwaite busied himself with getting the fire going, looking very much at home. Hardwick opened a gleaming mahogany cabinet to reveal a large variety of alcohol. He poured three brandies and carried them to a low table beside the fire.

Once the fire was blazing satisfactorily in the wide hearth, Braithwaite wriggled out of his coat and joined them on the chairs around the table. 'I want to hear *everything*,' he said.

Blake went through his escapades, from the unproductive meeting with Surridge to the escape from Zeb and Kagga. The other two listened intently, Hardwick with concentration and Braithwaite wide-eyed and excitable, giving the impression he was pigeonholing information, especially the gruesome bits, for his future novels.

'And that's it,' Blake finished, draining half his brandy in one gulp, wincing a little as the raw liquor stung the back of his throat.

'This is extraordinary! And you say that these two oddballs are still at large?' asked Braithwaite.

'Well, one of them would struggle to be classed as large, but yes. I don't know if they're still with the circus and I was in no mood to go looking for them.'

'Don't worry, Charles. We'll deal with them in due course,' said Hardwick. 'What I need from you is an opinion on this lot.' He opened his holdall and took out the statuette, the photographs and the driver's license.

Braithwaite immediately picked up the statuette, turning it over in his hands. 'This is interesting. Limestone that's been painted black. He's holding the crook and the flail, of course, but the headdress is a little unusual. I'll need to look that up.' He picked up the group photograph and studied it. 'So this is the infamous Mr Snell? He doesn't really look like a Black Ipsissimus, does he? And this one must be the unfortunate inhabitant of Jeremy's sarcophagus, or potential inhabitant I should say. I mustn't assume too much. The dwarf looks rather effective as Bes, doesn't he?' He peered intently at the photograph. 'It really is impossible to make out the other two, more's the pity.'

'We're lucky it survived at all . . . but the pièce de résistance is this.' Hardwick opened his bag again and handed Braithwaite the grimoire.

The horror writer gasped and took the book with shaking hands. 'Oh my God! Where did you find this?' he said hoarsely.

'It was on a shrine Snell had hidden in his basement and this picture of Lavelle was inside it.'

Braithwaite looked at the photograph. 'The inverted ankh,' he muttered. 'The Mark of Death! This is worse than I thought.' Taking the grimoire, he gently turned the pages, eyes flicking rapidly over the text. 'Now I see why you didn't want me to bring Jeremy tonight. Okay, let's approach this methodically. It's a corrupt version of *The Book of the Dead*. I say a corrupt version because whereas the original is known as *The Chapters of Coming Forth by Day* and were a New Kingdom collection of spells designed to assist the dead on the journey through the Duat — the afterlife — this is *The Chapters of Coming Forth by Night*. Very few copies of it are known to exist. I would guess this one is early eighteenth century, looking at the bindings. Written in Arabic, Latin and ancient Egyptian hieroglyphics, with illustrations that are highly suggestive of what we might call black magic.'

He looked up at the others. 'It was compiled principally for occultists, necromancers and sorcerers who wished to invoke evil spirits. The correct recitation of its passages were supposed to convey immortality and untold power on the reader, providing the rituals were executed in the proper manner. There's no doubt that Snell was experimenting with powerful stuff. If you put this together with the other happenings, and particularly with the fact that Jeremy's marked image was found in this book, it does look like he was up to no good. I don't suppose you know which page it was in?' He looked enquiringly at Blake.

'Sorry, no. Does it make a difference?'

'Possibly. I'll have to study this properly to know for sure. But if this is what I expect it is, then not only Jeremy's life, but his very soul, is in danger.'

8

The living room at Tanis Towers was silent except for the crackle and hiss of the fire. Blake examined Braithwaite's face, looking for signs that this was a joke. To his dismay, the man was completely serious.

Hardwick broke the silence. 'Do you think it's as bad as all that? I mean, we can keep Jeremy safe while we hunt down the bastards who are doing this. Hell, I could fly him out of the country; take him to the States.'

Braithwaite shook his head. 'That would protect his body right enough, but if their high priest — *new* high priest I should say, as Snell has been killed — has enough potency, they could work their spells even from a distance. His best chance is for us to be totally honest with him and work out what to do together. Do you think — '

'Excuse me, but I feel like I've entered

165

the *Twilight Zone* here!' Blake interrupted. The idea that what had started out as a murder investigation — admittedly a strange one — was now metamorphosising into something even weirder did not sit well with him. He was increasingly baffled by the unquestioning beliefs of these two grown men. How on earth could they take this stuff seriously? 'Have you any proof that this kind of magic actually works?' he asked.

Hardwick grunted irritably. 'You can't deny that there have been two murders connected with this already.'

'Murders, yes, and it's three. Remember Jennings?'

Hardwick brushed this aside. 'I don't think his death was of significance.'

Blake felt himself getting hot. 'Maybe not to you, but I bet it was significant to him!'

'Okay, keep your hair on. It was a bad choice of words. I meant that there's nothing other than the way he died to link him to this. He was unlucky enough to be in the wrong place at the wrong time. The point is that there are many reports of rituals of this kind being effective over the centuries. The ancients knew a lot more than most people give them credit for. The fact that Snell was seeing things is a strong indication that he became the focus of malign intention. Charles, has Jeremy had any more episodes since he's been at your home?' asked Hardwick.

'I'm afraid so. Just last night he swore he could see shapes moving around outside, but it's always been when my wife and I were in another room. I went to check on him about halfway through the night, as Henrietta thought she'd heard him speaking. He was moaning in his sleep and kept on saying, 'it's at Tanis Towers.' I woke him and we sat up together for an hour. I think being kept out of the loop won't do him any good. He needs to know what we're up against if we're going to have any hope in battling this thing.'

Hardwick threw another log on the fire while he deliberated. 'You may be right,' he eventually conceded.

'Good. I've been toying with an idea to bring whoever's doing this out into the open, and it would need Jeremy's co-operation. Do you remember the talk Professor Douglas gave us a few years ago on New Kingdom periapts and charms?'

'I was on a business trip and had to miss it but I know the one you mean. Sylvia said it was inspiring.'

'She's right. It was a brilliant, informative talk. He described how one could set up charms and prayers to create a circle of protection around oneself to ward off evil influences.' Braithwaite spoke quickly, the worry that had creased his brow now replaced with an intensity of purpose. 'I have the notes he handed out at home and I think, with a bit of preparation, we could do it.'

'It would be worth a try,' Hardwick agreed. 'But you said it would draw out whoever's responsible — how?'

'If we cut Jeremy off from their long-distance influence they'll have to try a direct approach on his life. They'll have to come out into the open!'

Blake had been listening to all of it with incredulity, but actually he quite liked Braithwaite's plan. If this lot were as superstitious as this, then a bit of

168

chanting and dancing or whatever it was should be reassuring for Lavelle and could not do any harm. If he could prod them into putting some safeguards in place, the idea of using Lavelle as bait could work. He had also pricked up his ears at the mention of Sylvia Black. He had forgotten about her, but could she be the female figure in the photograph? Since day one of this case he had held the idea that Lavelle's enemies could well be part of the Order — either past or present — or a splinter group thereof. 'Where would you perform this protective . . . ritual? At your house?' he asked.

'Actually, I'd suggest Tanis Towers. It has the right vibrations and we can include a cleansing spell to rid the place of any lingering effects of the unwrapping,' Braithwaite answered. 'I can see in your eyes that you don't share our faith. That matters not. What matters is that we believe it and know it for what it is. Magic can only be countered by magic and fortunately, now that we know what we're up against, we have the means of combating it.'

Had Blake's and Lavelle's positions been reversed, he knew he would far rather put his faith in something tangible — like a gun. For the time being, and especially in light of Hardwick's full support to this idea, he knew he would be best just shutting up and going along with it. 'And I take it you have to prepare for this? How long do you think it'll take?' he asked.

Braithwaite considered for a moment, tapping his fingers absently on the grimoire. 'If I work flat out we could be ready by tomorrow night.'

'As we're letting Jeremy in on this, he could help you. That would speed it up a bit, wouldn't it?' Hardwick said.

'Not a good idea, I'm afraid,' Braithwaite replied emphatically. 'Until the protective spells are in place, he'd be very vulnerable to emanations from the book itself.'

'Okay,' Blake said. 'I'd like to give this place a thorough check-over. If you're going to bring Lavelle here in the hope that it'll also bring out his attacker or attackers, we need to know that he's going to be safe. I wouldn't want you locking yourselves in with a bunch of murderous nutters just because you've forgotten about the cellar door or the skylight that doesn't shut properly. Can I get the key from you tomorrow?' he asked Hardwick.

'Why not keep it now? You can stay overnight and get straight to work,' Hardwick suggested with the faintest ghost of a smile on his lips.

Blake could not help remembering the words Lavelle had been saying in his sleep — 'It's at Tanis Towers' — and he had a brief feeling of anxiety. Pushing it down as ridiculous, he nodded his head. 'Sounds sensible. I don't really need anything from the office for this.'

They went over a few details, then Hardwick and Braithwaite departed, leaving Blake alone in the silent house.

★ ★ ★

An hour later, Blake had explored every room, from the cellar to the attic. There was even a door out to each of the turrets.

He supposed he could conceivably call them towers as Lavelle had done, but to him they were far more like the crenellated defences he had seen on castles; and each had a small, square external area from which the view over the lights of the city was impressive. Having made note of all the possible entry points and how they could be secured, he had rooted through Lavelle's cupboards for a hastily put-together meal and brought it to eat in the living room. It was the only room that was warm enough; and besides, it contained the drinks cabinet.

Sitting back on the sofa with a medicinal glass of brandy, he went over the case in his head. Leaving aside all the superstitious madness, which he did not believe for one moment, what had actually happened so far? Three people had been decapitated. Two of them had bought into a belief in magic and superstition. The third appeared to have been very unlucky and got in the way of the murderer or murderers. Then there were the things that Lavelle believed he had seen, here at Tanis Towers, that had freaked him out. From what he could make out, there had been nothing that could not have been faked, particularly by two people who worked in a circus and might be used to special effects. The floating head outside the kitchen window might actually have been Ryan's, hanging by fishing wire from a long pole. It would look horrible enough to discourage Lavelle from going to investigate.

It seemed strange to him that there had not been an attempt to kill Lavelle at that point. Was all of this just geared to scare him . . . to drive him mad? Or was the 'haunting' the two characters' idea — to have a bit of fun freaking out their victim? Whatever the case, he was certain that Zeb and Kagga had killed Jennings, so it was likely that they were involved in all three murders. However, he found it hard to believe that those two nutcases were working on their own. Even if Zeb did participate in the rituals, as the photograph suggested, he guessed it was due more to his morphology than his intelligence and mystical beliefs.

Braithwaite had taken the photograph with him as he and Hardwick were going to let Lavelle know all that had happened, but Blake had studied the photograph several times that day and he was certain that the obscured male figure was not Kagga, who was taller and thinner. So who exactly were the other two in the group photograph? Were *they* responsible for the deaths, or were they next in line for the chop? There had been no other decapitations reported recently, but without knowing their identity he could not be sure if they were alive or dead.

Deciding he had lounged about for long enough, Blake pushed himself up from the sofa. Time to get on with his real purpose in getting access to Lavelle's house. The study was impressive with its many ancient Egyptian artefacts and row upon row of books on Egyptology; but the really interesting room, as far as he was concerned, was a plain, modern one on the first floor which housed filing cabinets with all the affairs of the Order neatly documented within.

He set to work sifting through the

subscription details, the costs and profits of the conferences and lectures the Order had organised, and the expenses that Lavelle had claimed for over the years. The picture slowly formed of a surprisingly well-run society that provided a very tidy income for its founder. Whether or not Lavelle believed his own hype, he would die rich at this rate.

Blake checked his watch. It was already coming up to midnight, but he wanted to get this part of the work done tonight. It was possible that Hardwick might appear in the morning and he did not really want a witness to his research. He was working on the members now. He had a column of names and the years in which they had joined. He also noticed there were two types of membership — a basic one that was fairly costly and a gold subscription that granted access to all of the Order's events, publications and meetings, including ones solely for gold subscribers. This was seriously expensive and there were only a few people who had bought it, namely Jeremy Lavelle, Sylvia Black, Don Hardwick, Charles Braithwaite and Larry

Williams — the inner-circle members.

He saw that the Order had been founded eleven years ago and that Braithwaite had joined in the first few months. It had been three years later that Hardwick and Black had signed up and Hardwick had immediately taken over the financial side of things. Was it just coincidence that both had joined within the same week? Copies of letters chasing payments became far more professional, as did the ledger in which the details were kept. It was clear that Hardwick contributed more than just money, having spent a considerable amount of time recruiting members and even promoting the Order overseas. Blake flicked through the details, working forward to the present day, and was interested to see that recently the momentum seemed to have been slowing down. In the last two years there had been no new subscriptions taken out.

Crouching over the filing cabinets was beginning to strain his back and he straightened up, wincing slightly. His eyes ached as well and he took a decision to leave things for tonight. He would try to make sense of the information in the morning. There were several guest bedrooms but they were all chilly and lifeless. It did not look like Lavelle had many visitors; in fact he had the impression that the man only used a few rooms in the house regularly.

Gathering up a pillow and some blankets, Blake made himself up a bed on the sofa next to the fire in the living room. In spite of being used to sleeping in this rough and ready fashion, he had a fitful night, and several times he dreamed of being trapped in the cellar of Snell's house while a maelstrom of fire raged above him and a leering dwarf, dressed in an impish costume, cavorted in the flames, a bloody, severed head in his hand.

*　★　*

The pale winter sunlight slanted in through a gap in the curtains and woke Blake up. He had slept later than he had intended and found he was stiff and bruised from the exertions of the day before. Questions were lining up in his head, waiting for answers he probably could not provide as yet. He stretched painfully and then gave the ashes in the grate a prod, hoping to bring the fire back to life. There was a dimly glowing log left and he coaxed it with paper and kindling until the fire was burning steadily.

He tidied away his bedding and had a quick wash then went to the kitchen to find coffee and toast. A radio would have been welcome too. This place was set back quite a distance from the road and felt much more remote than it actually was. A cheery morning-radio broadcaster would have made him feel less divorced from the rest of the city. He took his breakfast through to the dining room and sat at the long table to eat, looking at the photographs on the walls. Lavelle was in most of them, but he recognised Hardwick and Braithwaite too and even spotted Surridge in one, looking far more dramatic with a different haircut and a goatee.

One of the photographs showed the Sphinx in the background with a group of people in the foreground. He got up for a closer look. In the centre were Lavelle, Hardwick and a striking woman with jet-black hair and a voluptuous figure that Jane Russell might have envied. That had to be Sylvia Black. Once he had spotted her he picked her out in several others, always near the two men. He decided he needed to talk to her next; after all, it was traditional for private investigators to meet sultry women who were probably bad news. So far the closest he had got was the bearded lady at the circus camp. The thought brought a wry smile to his face.

Finishing the last bite of toast, Blake got out his notebook and began to plan his day. He should check out the grounds now that it was light enough to do so, and he wanted to sound the others out about getting in some hired muscle to be on hand in case of a direct attempt on Lavelle's life. He should either go to see Sylvia or telephone her, and he needed to know when Braithwaite would be ready to bring Lavelle back to Tanis Towers and put his plan into action.

Deciding to tackle the grounds first, Blake searched the extensive garden thoroughly. Although there was a high wall behind the trees, it would not be that difficult for intruders to climb over, and even easier for someone to sneak down the drive after dark. Once in the garden there were plenty of places to hide in the bushes. They would definitely need to be vigilant. He had debated whether to advise Hardwick to bite the bullet and call the police. To at least report Zeb and Kagga for their murder of Jennings and attempted murder of a certain private investigator. The problem was that he knew at least a part of Hardwick's success was founded on fraudulent practices. When he had started working for the American he had done a little digging, just for his own security, and he was sure that any official investigation was bound to open up a whole can of slimy things. His own sporadic work for Hardwick would come under scrutiny too, and though he was pretty sure he would weather the storm with a caution, it was not something he would welcome. If this could be done on the sly then all the better . . . for everyone concerned.

The idea that Braithwaite could install some kind of defensive charm and that Lavelle's enemy would be aware of it was ridiculous. However if, as he suspected, Zeb and Kagga had plagued the man the last time he was here, it was quite possible they could try again once their victim was alone. He could suggest that they brought Lavelle here and then pretended to leave. Then, if an attack happened, they would be on hand.

Sitting at the desk in Lavelle's office, he dialled the number for Hardwick. As he waited for the phone to be answered his eyes fell on the sarcophagus that had started all this and he wondered how it would all end. He found himself thinking just how strangely everything had panned out, reflecting over the idea of some ancient Egyptian undertaker — or whatever the equivalent had been — having no concept whatsoever about where his coffin would end up and to what use it would be put.

'Good morning. How can I help you?' a

bright female voice sounded in his ear.

'I'd like to speak to Mr Hardwick. It's Adam Blake.'

'I'm sorry, but Mr Hardwick's not due in the office until one o'clock. Can I take a message?'

'It's okay, I'll call back.' Blake hung up and tried Hardwick's home number. The housekeeper answered and shortly Hardwick came on the line. 'Blake?' he said.

'Yes. How did it go with Lavelle last night?'

'All right, I guess. He was pretty calm about it. He seems to have got some of his nerve back. He's agreed for us all to meet up at Tanis Towers tonight at ten o'clock. Braithwaite figures he should be ready by then.'

'I've thoroughly checked the house and grounds and I'd strongly advise getting in a few men to be on hand just in case there's an attack.'

'Could do. I'd feel happier with some tangible back-up, but if we're trying to draw out the enemy we can't exactly have armed guards around.'

'There are several places we could

conceal a couple of men, both inside and outside. I've got some ideas about that. Do you want me to hire some?'

'No, I'll do that,' Hardwick said. 'I want you to stay put there — make sure no one tries to sneak in. I'll let you know what's happening.'

'Actually, I was hoping to get in touch with Sylvia Black and Larry Williams. I haven't got their thoughts on all this,' Blake said.

'Don't bother about them.' Hardwick was firm. 'Larry just wants to be left out of it. Sylvia knows what I know. I've talked to her myself. She doesn't have anything to add.'

'I really think it would be worth — '

'Drop it, Blake. I want you there. Stay where you can hear the phone.' Hardwick rang off.

'Well that's me told,' Blake said to himself, putting the phone down, resigning himself to what looked like being a boring day. Still, Hardwick was paying him well to sit around. He spent a little time writing up his expenses, then went for a wander round the house. It was a pretty big place for a man living on his own. He had seen from Lavelle's expenses that he charged the Order for a cleaner who came in every other day. Presumably she had been paid off for the moment, as dust was beginning to settle on everything. No sign of a housekeeper like Hardwick had.

Rooting through the kitchen cupboards and the freezer, Blake could tell that Lavelle did not do much cooking. There did not seem to be any sign of a Mrs Lavelle, either past or present, and there had been no mention of any family. He perked up. If he had to be stuck here he could at least take the opportunity to find out everything he could about Lavelle. His previous searches had been into the business, but now he was looking for personal information.

Walking back down the corridor to the study, he admired the entry hall. It was high and wide with the sweeping staircase opposite the ornate front door. Climbing the stairs, he went straight to Lavelle's bedroom and began shamelessly rummaging through everything. There were a large wardrobe and two chests of drawers full of good-quality clothing, some of which had to be costumes for the Order's ceremonial occasions. The double bed was still rumpled from the last night Lavelle had spent there and he left that alone. There were a few photographs on the mantelpiece, mostly taken in exotic places, but there were two that looked more commonplace. One showed a couple on their wedding day. He turned it over and saw a handwritten date on the back: 5th May 1919. Perhaps Lavelle's father had just come back from the Great War and married his sweetheart. He could make out a resemblance. The other photograph was of a young man in a black gown and mortarboard — Lavelle at Oxford before he got kicked out.

The bedside table was Blake's next target. Sitting on the edge of the bed, he pulled out the drawer and rested it on the bed. There were handkerchiefs, a small packet of boiled sweets, and an envelope. Disregarding the rest, he opened this and found several handwritten letters. Blake felt his pulse quicken. They were all from

Sylvia Black. He skimmed through them to get the gist of the correspondence, then let out an explosive breath. Working quickly, he put the letters in date order.

The first was from eight years ago and was really a fan letter. Sylvia had read all his articles and hoped very much that they could meet. The next must have been sent after she had joined the Order, as it referred to the excitement of meeting others like herself. And so it went on. By the fourth letter, she was writing about a trip the Order was planning to Egypt and how she hoped there would be some time for private conversation away from the others.

Blake chuckled to himself. Maybe Lavelle was not quite as much of a loner as he looked. He swung his feet up on the bed and read unashamedly through the letters. There had definitely been something between the two of them over the years. As the letters became more recent, he noticed a slight change of tone. The effusive praise had changed to more of a shared discussion of ideas, with even the occasional criticism. Either Sylvia was becoming disillusioned or just more confident about speaking her mind. The last letter, dated ten months ago, made him sit up. Sylvia was chiding Lavelle for jealousy and impatience, telling him to bide his time. She did not mention any names but wrote of a 'dear friend of many years' who would be upset by any mention of their relationship.

Leafing through the letters, Blake searched them for any clue to this 'dear friend', but there was nothing. She must have assumed that Lavelle would know immediately who she was referring to. He cursed himself. He had not even thought about a love triangle but if Sylvia had another man, be it a husband or lover, then he could be responsible for this whole mess. Of all the cases he had worked on in over twenty years, spurned lovers were the most vindictive.

He took the letters downstairs and picked up the telephone in the hall. To his frustration, Hardwick had left home but not reached his office yet. What about Braithwaite? Maybe he would know something. Consulting his notebook, he found the telephone number for the horror writer's home, which he had copied down when he had last been there, and dialled it. It was engaged.

Frustrated, Blake tried the number several times but still no luck. There had been no telephone number for Sylvia in the files, just an address on the other side of the city. Cursing the fact that he was pinned down at Tanis Towers, he sat down in the living room and tried to work out what they would do in the unlikely circumstance that tonight's events actually caught anyone. How on earth were they going to deal with one or more murderers if they were not to be handed over to the authorities? He did not believe that Hardwick or Lavelle would have the inclination to become killers themselves, although he could be wrong. More likely they would cave in and present the police with a highly edited story. One that left out the mummy altogether. Hardwick might offer a substantial bribe for the perpetrators to talk only about Snell's death. Blake shook his head. Personally he could not see it working.

Standing up, he paced impatiently over to the window. The best thing he could do was try to earn his wages. He had been called in to discover who the corpse was and if there was a threat to Lavelle or the Order. Well, he had done that. He would help out tonight, but there was no way he was going to assist with anything more dubious. If they decided to hang the consequences and call the police in, he would give his evidence with a fairly clear conscience.

The sound of footsteps on gravel caught his attention. Stepping quickly to the window, he saw a postman coming down the drive. Relaxing the muscles he had involuntarily tensed, he went to the front door and waited for the post to flop through the letterbox. He was getting too jumpy. The post joined yesterday's uncollected letters in the wire basket that hung from the letterbox. This had been hidden by the plush velvet curtains which hung on either side of the front door and Blake fished out all the post. There were two magazines and a couple of bills, but the one that caught his eye was a small envelope in handwriting he had come to recognise — Sylvia Black's.

He wondered whether to steam it open so he could re-seal it later but then shrugged and opened it anyway. It might be important, and he could deal with any indignation Lavelle might feel. It was a brief letter. She had been trying to call him, to see how the investigation was going. The whole thing had upset her dreadfully and she wished they could be together, but he must understand the difficulties she faced. She ended by begging him to contact her.

Interesting, but not really illuminating, Blake thought as he put the letter back with the other post. It was getting on for lunchtime but he decided to try Hardwick and Braithwaite again. Hardwick had still not turned up at his office but Braithwaite's phone was finally free.

'Adder Brook House,' answered a voice he recognised as Mrs Braithwaite's.

'Can I speak to Mr Lavelle or Mr Braithwaite please? It's Adam Blake, the investigator.'

'I'm afraid Jeremy is resting and I really

don't want to disturb him, but Charles is just in his study. I'll get him for you.'

There was a long pause and then the sound of footsteps.

'Braithwaite here.'

'Mr Braithwaite, it's Adam Blake.'

'Ah, hello. I'm getting on quite well with the book.'

'That's not what I'm calling about. Can I ask you some questions about Sylvia Black?'

'Sylvia! Yes, of course.'

'Did you know that she and Lavelle were involved with each other?' Blake asked baldly.

'*Sylvia and Jeremy?* Whatever makes you think that?' Braithwaite said in astonishment.

Blake explained about the letters and Braithwaite listened with only the occasional question. When he had finished there was silence at the other end of the line. 'Mr Braithwaite? Are you there?'

'Yes . . . I'm still here. Look, Blake, are you certain of your facts? You're sure Sylvia and Jeremy were intending to pair up sometime in the near future?'

'I am. I'd have called Hardwick but he's out. Perhaps he knows more about it.'

'No! For God's sake don't do that!' Braithwaite exclaimed.

'Why?'

'Haven't you realised? The other man, the 'dear friend' — it's him, Hardwick!'

9

It took Blake several seconds to realise that Braithwaite was still talking. His mind had frozen at the revelation that Hardwick *could* be the killer.

' . . . known her for years before they joined the Order. I'm afraid he doesn't like to talk about it and I wasn't aware that Jeremy knew. She's married but her husband is much older than her and very ill. I'd always rather assumed she and Don would eventually get together. If Sylvia's going to take up with Jeremy, marry him even, it would break Don's heart.'

'Or perhaps his mind!' Blake was feeling the adrenaline rush he always got when there was finally a breakthrough in a case. 'Wait a minute though. If Hardwick still holds a torch for Sylvia and has done all of this to get Lavelle out of the way, it leaves a lot of questions. I mean, why go to such great lengths? If he wanted to kill him, why not just do it rather than create this complicated plot that incidentally resulted in the deaths of three other people? It's not logical.'

'Maybe the plan is to unhinge Jeremy, not to kill him. Maybe those others had crossed him in some way unrelated to this,' Braithwaite suggested.

'Perhaps. But what about bringing me in to investigate? That was *his* suggestion, wasn't it?'

'Yes, and think about it — that was a clever move. You work for him. He can order you around and he'll always know what you're doing. He would've had none of that if the police were involved, now, would he?'

Blake thought furiously. If one were going to commit murder, then being in control of the investigation would undoubtedly be a huge help. Hardwick was a man used to getting his own way in life. If he had been in love with Sylvia and was expecting her to marry him once her elderly husband was dead, to then find out that she was seeing Jeremy would be a huge blow to his ego. All the same, he didn't feel inclined to judge Hardwick completely on what amounted to rumour. He needed to talk to the man in person, make up his own mind.

'I really think I ought to take Jeremy somewhere that Don doesn't know about,' Braithwaite said, anxiety making his voice higher than normal. 'Hopefully I'm wrong, but I can't risk Don coming here if he really has lost his mind. Or sending those awful men, the dwarf and the axe-thrower.'

'You could go to the police. Tell them that there have been death threats or something.'

'That wouldn't be wise. They can only protect his physical body.' Braithwaite sounded determined.

Blake ground his teeth with frustration. 'Well if you won't do that, then moving to a new location might not be a bad idea. I'm going to see if I can find Hardwick and show him the letters from Sylvia. His reaction to seeing them should tell me a lot. When I know where we stand, I'll let you know.'

'All right. I'll wait to hear from you.'

Braithwaite seemed to be signing off.

'Hang on! I need to know how to reach you.'

'Oh. Yes, of course.' There was silence for a few seconds. 'I don't know exactly where we will go. There are a few possibilities. I'd better leave you a note. Did you see the sundial in my garden?'

'On the front lawn? Yes.'

'Good. I'll leave a message just behind the base of that. I must go; there's a lot to do.' Braithwaite put the phone down.

Blake gathered up the love letters from Sylvia to Lavelle and put them in a jacket pocket. He quickly locked up the house and then phoned Hardwick's office. A secretary informed him that Hardwick had called to say he would not be coming in after all. He dialled the home number. As usual the housekeeper answered. This time he was in luck. Hardwick was expected back at any minute. He did not bother to leave any message and set off to confront the man he worked for.

★ ★ ★

Heavy rain clouds had dimmed the sky and Blake put his headlights on. It was quite a drive to Hardwick's house, which was in the countryside to the north of the city. Blake had only been there once before but he could remember the way well enough. As he drove, he thought over the problem of what to do if Hardwick was the man behind the murders. The main solution was obvious — he would report him to the police. Well aware that things could turn nasty, he took comfort from the blackjack in his pocket.

Blake turned the car into the wide driveway of the country house, the beams of his headlights illuminating the warm limestone walls of the building. He noted the presence of Hardwick's Ford Zephyr with a mixture of apprehension and determination. Time for the showdown — one way or another he would get some answers.

Leaving his car, he rang the doorbell. The housekeeper opened the door. 'Hello,' she said politely. Blake had seen her on the previous occasion he had been here but she clearly did not remember him.

'Adam Blake, to see Mr Hardwick.'

She recognised his name at least and he was shown into the house. Waiting in one of the reception rooms he stood by the window, watching the fading light outside and preparing himself mentally for the interview.

Hardwick strode in, looking annoyed. 'What're you doing here, Blake? I told you to stay put.'

Blake sat down on one of the sofas. 'There's been a development and I couldn't get hold of you either at the office or here,' he said calmly.

'All right then. What've you got for me?' Hardwick took a seat opposite Blake, his tone and body language still belligerent.

'You might find these interesting . . . I know I did.' Blake extracted the letters from his jacket and handed them over, watching Hardwick intently.

The American looked at the first letter and his eyes widened, scanning quickly through it. After the third letter there was a slight smile on his lips.

Blake interrupted his reading. 'What do

you make of them?' he asked.

'It's pretty obvious, isn't it? They had a thing for each other. I hadn't picked this up, but thinking back on things it makes sense. Sylvia married Joseph Black when she was twenty-two and completely broke. I'm sure she's fond of him. He's a decent guy but she's still young, and if they want to get together after he's snuffed it then good luck to them.'

Hardwick sounded genuine and Blake was fairly sure it was not acting, but he pressed on. 'But who do you think is the 'dear friend' that she mentions? The one who would be really hurt by their relationship.'

'Joseph, naturally. He's been in bad health for years and I'd reckon there's less than a year left for him. I don't think he'd begrudge Sylvia another husband, but it's not really something she'd want to bring up now, is it? Jeremy will just have to wait a bit.' Hardwick's face clouded over again. 'We've got to get him out of this mess and I don't see how these letters constitute a development.'

Blake was almost convinced now that

Braithwaite had got it wrong, but he had to be sure. 'I heard that you wanted Sylvia for yourself,' he said bluntly.

Hardwick's eyebrows shot up in astonishment. 'Who the hell told you that? I've known Sylvia for years. She helped me get set up in England when I first came over here. She's a good friend but there's never been anything like that between us.' His eyes narrowed thoughtfully. 'Who told you there was?'

Blake hesitated. He was thinking back over the conversation with Braithwaite and starting to worry. Hardwick's story and reaction was ringing true according to all the experience he had gained over the years listening to liars. He started to explain. 'When I found those letters it immediately suggested a new angle to the case, one that I hadn't even considered. Sylvia is so keen that her 'dear friend' does not hear about her feelings for Lavelle that I started to wonder if there was an entirely different motive for these murders. That a jealous husband or lover was targeting Lavelle.'

'Joseph certainly doesn't fit the bill.

He's bedbound and can't speak and he's been like that for over a year. But you said you thought it could be me?' Hardwick considered the concept, his chin set and eyes hard. 'Okay, I think I can see your point. If I *had* been after Sylvia, then finding out that she intended to get together with Jeremy would've been a big thing. The fact remains that you still haven't told me who's been blackening my name. Have you been talking to Surridge again?'

Blake took a deep breath. 'Actually, when I couldn't get hold of you to ask about Sylvia, I called Braithwaite and he was certain that you two were . . . involved.'

'*What?* He knows that's nonsense. Why would he say that? I'll call him up. You must have misunderstood.' Hardwick got up and headed for the hallway.

Blake followed. 'Wait. He's probably not there.'

'Don't be an idiot, of course he's there. He's got to keep an eye on Jeremy.' Hardwick brushed Blake's objection aside.

'*Don!*' Blake used his employer's name for the first time he could remember.

201

'Braithwaite was convinced that you were the one who's out to get Lavelle. He told me point-blank that you were in love with Sylvia and were trying to send your rival nuts.'

Hardwick had stopped walking and turned to look incredulously at Blake. 'Are you sure he said all of that?'

'Positive. He was pretty convinced and unless he answers his phone now, he and Lavelle will have up and left for a different location.'

Thinking hard, Hardwick began chewing the inside of his cheek. He picked up the telephone in the hall and dialled a number. After forty seconds there was no answer and he slowly put the receiver down. 'He really believes it was me,' he said quietly. 'When we met and explained it all to Jeremy last night I impressed how important it was that we kept in contact. I said that I was going to arrange a late flight out of the country for Jeremy after Braithwaite had done his stuff with the talismans.' He looked a little embarrassed. 'I'll admit I didn't really buy the idea of magical protection, but I do know that the mind can be a powerful thing; and if Jeremy believed he was protected, it would give him a boost while I put the Atlantic Ocean between him and trouble.'

'You've got a flight booked? And Braithwaite knew this?' Blake asked, the tiniest hint of suspicion beginning to form.

'Yes. It's for quarter-past midnight. I've arranged for him to stay with a cousin of mine, but I can't get him to the airport with his tickets if I don't know where he is.'

Blake was silent. Memories and impressions were coalescing in his head — Braithwaite's reaction on seeing the grimoire; his insistence that Lavelle was safe with him; the hint of contempt when he was looking at the picture of Snell; and most of all, one small comment about Zeb and Kagga.

'When I was telling you about the fight at Snell's house, did I take you through it blow by blow, or did I just say there was a fight?'

'What's this got to do with anything?' Hardwick protested impatiently.

'Please. Just tell me. What did I tell you and Braithwaite about the fight?'

'Okay!' Hardwick thought for a moment. 'I can't remember exactly, but I think you said you got discovered by the dwarf, then were jumped from behind by the other one. You struggled and ended up getting away from them briefly. Then you got shut in the hidden basement and the dwarf tried to burn you alive.'

'Did I tell you what the taller man was armed with?' Blake asked intently.

Hardwick concentrated. 'I really don't think so,' he finally said. 'I know you said he was ugly, scarred and had a ring through his nose like a bull, but I honestly can't remember you talking about a weapon.'

'Tonight on the phone, Braithwaite described him as an axe-thrower — which is true, but I really don't think I mentioned it. How could he have known?'

Hardwick started towards the front door, looking grim. 'I can see where you're going with this and I don't like it. Let's go to Adder Brook. I want some answers.'

'Braithwaite said he'd leave me a note

there of where they've gone. If he has, then we've been overreacting. We'll explain that he was wrong about you and we can get Jeremy on that plane.'

'If there's no note, then he's been manipulating us all along.' Hardwick strode out of the house. Seeing Blake heading for his own car, Hardwick grabbed his arm. 'Leave that old banger. My car will get us there far faster.'

★ ★ ★

Rain drummed steadily on the roof of the car, running in tiny rivulets down the windscreen where the wiper was working overtime, desperately trying to clear them away. The road in front was a mirror-like stretch of water reflecting the powerful headlights. Half an hour later they made the turnoff, heading down the track.

Passing one of the neighbouring houses, which was set some distance away, Blake found himself wondering what the other residents of the small hamlet would think if they knew what might be going on in their midst. It was a facet of crime which had always intrigued him: the realisation that no one really knew for sure just what went on behind closed doors. Not that long ago he had gone to the cinema with an ex-girlfriend to watch *10 Rillington Place*, a crime-drama film about the life and murderous exploits of John Christie within what was called 'The Original House of Horrors', and was stunned as to how no one living nearby was aware of the terrible things going on inside. Had Number Three Adder Brook become something similar?

'We're here,' said Hardwick. He brought the car to a standstill.

Blake leaned forward in his seat and looked through the windscreen at Braithwaite's house, seeing that there were no lighted windows visible from the front. For a fleeting moment fear was strong within him and he felt a sick apprehension in the pit of his stomach. Consciously, he pushed it down and tried to ignore it.

'His car's not here,' noted Hardwick grimly.

Darkness had fallen and the rain and hail that had impeded their journey had now ceased their insane lashing. There was a thin crescent moon hanging low over the nearby trees, just visible between patches of tattered cloud which raced across it.

'Okay, let's do this.' Hardwick opened his door, got out and, in true mobster fashion, turned up his coat collar.

On the journey here it had been decided that if Braithwaite and Jeremy were not there and if there were no message by the sundial, Blake would break in and see what he could find, while Hardwick would remain outside on the lookout for trouble.

Clinging to the shadows and using whatever cover he could, Blake, jemmy in hand, walked towards the sundial. It was on the lawn just as he remembered but there was no sign of any note. He checked thoroughly in case a piece of paper could have blown away, but he was sure there had never been one. He shook his head to let Hardwick know.

Going round to the rear of the house, he tried the handle of the back door, unsurprised to find it locked. Head low, he made his way around the rear of the building, searching for a viable window. He soon found one which he considered appropriate and, wedging the small crowbar into place, began to prise it up. Housebreaking had become an almost routine part of his job under Hardwick and it was something which never ceased to send a thrill of excitement through him. He knew it was highly illegal, but then again much of what his employer asked of him fell into the same category or at the very least danced around its fringes.

From somewhere outside in the garden an owl hooted, the noise sending little shivers down his spine.

Tucking the jemmy into his belt, Blake clambered through the open window. Quietly, he got to his feet and lowered it once more. He peered around the shadowy room, its myriad contents little more than darkened blurs. The smell of furniture polish filled the air. In the dark and the silence, he waited and listened.

Having been here before, Blake reckoned that he was in Braithwaite's study.

Taking a torch from an inner jacket pocket, he switched it on, confirming his belief. Numerous bookshelves lined the walls and there was a large wooden desk at one end, atop which was a typewriter, sheets of paper, half a dozen paperbacks, all manner of stationery, and several small ancient Egyptian figurines of the kind he had seen at Lavelle's place. None of the latter were black like the one he had found in Snell's secret basement.

There were also several large filing cabinets, the contents of which, had he the time to investigate, would surely provide interesting reading. Now was not the time however. Right now the main priority was to find Lavelle and get him out of danger. Everything else could wait for another day.

Edging his way to the door on the far side, Blake thought he heard a sound coming from one of the rooms above. He stopped, straining his senses.

A dull thud sounded from directly overhead. It was followed by the barely audible sound of jingling bells.

Zeb!

A mental image of the sadistic midget in his dirty medieval jester's costume flashed through Blake's mind. His fingers tightened around the torch. Anger gleamed in his eyes. He had a score to settle with that short-arse. Like a venomous snake ready for the kill, he slid from the study out into a carpeted corridor which ran the length of the ground floor. To his right was the main entrance hall; to his left the doors to the lounge, the kitchen and the parlour. He paused before proceeding. Apart from the dull ticking of a grandfather clock, all was quiet.

Blake was now entering the main hall. In the beam of light thrown by his torch, he could see the wooden stairs leading to the upper floor. Gold-framed mirrors reached to the ceiling, glinting in the torchlight, and a large chandelier hung from above. Directly before him was the front door, beyond which he expected Hardwick to be stood on the lookout. Coming to the sensible decision that he could use some support if things were to turn nasty, he went to the door, unbolted it and pushed it open.

Hardwick stepped from the shadows, ready to pounce. He pulled back upon seeing Blake. 'You're lucky I didn't bring a gun. I could've shot you,' he cautioned.

'I think the mad dwarf's upstairs,' Blake whispered. 'He's nuts. I think it'd be best if we both went in.'

'No sign of Lavelle . . . or Braithwaite?'

'No. I guess they've gone.' Blake threw a sudden backward glance at the stairs. He thought he had heard something but there was nothing to be seen.

'Okay.' Hardwick came inside, closing the door behind him. He had no sooner turned when a throwing axe came flying out of the darkness, catching his coat sleeve and embedding itself into the door, effectively pinning him to it.

'*Jesus Christ!* Look out!' yelled Blake.

Screaming like a man possessed, Kagga leapt down the stairs, brandishing a second hand-axe. He came at a rush, swinging his weapon.

Ducking, Blake pulled back, narrowly avoiding being scalped. Frantically, he darted to one side. Grabbing a vase, he threw it at his mad-eyed assailant, cursing as the other easily dodged it. He could see Hardwick struggling to free himself. And then the hand-axe was coming straight for his face. Instinctively he got his left arm up, catching the other by the wrist.

There was a feral, insane look in Kagga's eyes. He drew his lips back, exposing his cracked, yellowed teeth. Spit drooled from the corner of his mouth.

Blake fought to maintain his grip, knowing that if he should lose his hold he risked getting his head cleaved in two. From this distance he could almost taste the man's halitosis. Savagely, he threw in an uppercut which smacked into Kagga's jaw. He did it again and again, each blow snapping back his would-be murderer's head.

It was all happening so fast. One minute they were grappling for possession of the sharp-bladed weapon, the next the two of them were crashing to the floor.

Having now disentangled himself from his coat, Hardwick ran over. Knowing that this bedlamite had to be disarmed, he brought his strength to bear on Kagga's arm, twisting it back, forcing him to release the weapon. Smacking in another punch, Blake then got to his feet. He bent down and retrieved the hand-axe.

Hardwick tightened his grip. 'I'll keep a hold of him. There's some rope in my car. We should tie the — ' Before he could finish his sentence, Kagga twisted madly, slipping free of his grip. With the agility of a wild cat, he launched himself to his feet and sank his teeth into the back of the American's left wrist. He cursed volubly and began to beat at the maniac with his free hand.

Blake was in two minds about using the hand-axe to just set about butchering the long-haired character but, throwing the weapon to one side, he decided to grab him instead. Gripping him in a tight stranglehold, he heaved him off his employer and wrestled him to the ground once more, only now remembering the blackjack in his jacket pocket. Thrashing like a crocodile, Kagga tried in vain to escape.

'I've got the bastard! Go and get the bloody rope!' Blake yelled, knowing full well that a strong sedative, a protective mouth guard and a straitjacket would be far more appropriate.

A stream of foreign words spewed from between Kagga's lips.

Massaging his bitten arm, Hardwick turned. A grim smile creased his face. He then called back in the same language.

For the next thirty seconds or so they traded insults in words that meant nothing to Blake. Finally, Hardwick went out and returned a minute later with a coil of rope.

'Right. Start with his feet,' said the private investigator, holding Kagga down. 'I take it you know what he's saying?'

Hardwick nodded. 'My mother's Hungarian, same as him. Although at eighty-seven, I doubt she's what he says she is.' Fiercely, he turned Kagga over and bound his arms behind his back, trussing him up like a turkey. Job done, he got to his feet.

Blake's thoughts turned to Zeb. Where the hell was he? Was he indeed here, or had he only imagined hearing the jingling bells? Knowing that subterfuge was no longer required, he went over and switched on the main hall lights. The child-sized motley lay halfway up the stairs but there was no sign of its owner. Perhaps Kagga had been toying with the idea of wearing it or had been taking it to be cleaned. He guessed anything was possible when it came to understanding the mind of a psychopath. Confident that the Hungarian madman was now incapacitated, and assured that Hardwick was keeping guard over him, he set about searching the house.

It was empty. There was no sign of Lavelle or either of the Braithwaites. Blake came down the stairs and reported as much to the American.

Hardwick crouched down, removed a pen from an inner jacket pocket and inserted it through his captive's nosering. He gave a sharp tug, his improvised torture method rewarded with a yelp of pain and a string of expletives. He then took out his cigarette lighter. With a flick of his thumb, an orange-tipped flame appeared. 'Okay, let's see if we can get our friend here to tell us where Braithwaite's taken Lavelle,' he said menacingly.

10

It was a twenty-minute drive to Tanis Towers and, certainly after the information Hardwick had extracted from Kagga, Blake knew time was of the essence. The interrogation had proceeded in Hungarian with the occasional bit of broken English. If the mad axe-thrower was to be believed, then Lavelle was going to be ritualistically slaughtered.

Blake had found it extremely hard to accept, but the story had gradually come out that Braithwaite had spent decades with Snell working on the spells contained in the grimoire. Both men fervently believed that if done correctly these incantations would imbue them with magical potency.

In the face of disbelief from his captors, Kagga had been adamant that the spells would work with the right sacrifice. Snell's experiments with circus animals had been disappointing, but when they killed Ryan there had been a glimpse of real power. Even as an onlooker, Kagga had felt it.

Hardwick had grown angrier as the interrogation had progressed. The betrayal of friendship that Braithwaite had planned was monstrous and calculated. It emerged that it had been the horror writer's insidious suggestion to get a mummy to unwrap, but he had done it so subtly that even Lavelle had not realised the idea had been planted. In fact, that had been the final confirmation of his guilt.

Directed by Kagga, Hardwick had found the headless remains of Aj-Merak secreted in an outhouse in the garden. The desiccated body had been partially destroyed to get mummia, which he imagined Braithwaite and his equally insane wife snorting like cocaine. At the point when Kagga had admitted that Lavelle was to be killed, he had started battering his captive seriously, demanding to know where they had taken him. Blake had needed to stop him from knocking the man unconscious or worse. Bleeding and snivelling, Kagga had finally told them the ritual was to take place at Tanis

Towers that night. They had left him tied and gagged in the downstairs bathroom where no one was likely to hear him.

'So how long do you think Braithwaite's had his eye on Lavelle?' Blake had asked once they were in the car.

'Could be as long as he's known him, but there's been a slight shift in the last two years. Charles has been encouraging Jeremy to see himself as a kind of spiritual leader of the Order. I thought it was just part of his general desire to push the esoteric side of ancient Egyptian studies, but it must have been to do with this.'

'I don't get it,' Blake confessed.

'You know some religions include the sacrifice of animals and sometimes humans?' Hardwick answered impatiently.

'Yes, I've heard of that,' replied Blake hesitantly.

'Well, to put it simply, the bigger the thing you're asking for the more important the sacrifice has to be. Braithwaite probably feels that the leader of the Order of the True Sphinx is the best he can get his hands on.'

'Doesn't mean much to me. As far as

I'm concerned, mad is mad. Anyway, how do you want to do things when we get there?' Blake asked tensely.

'What do you think? A direct assault on the place?'

'Personally, I'd suggest stealth. See exactly what's going on and how many there are. For all we know, Braithwaite might have a small army of his nutters gathered inside.'

'I'd be surprised if he's managed to get other people involved. My bet is that it'll just be the three of them. Don't forget his wife, Henrietta,' Hardwick cautioned. 'Our friend back at Braithwaite's said that she's in on it too.'

'All the same, I can't see her putting up much resistance. Same goes for Braithwaite. What are they, late sixties?'

'He's seventy. I know because I was at his birthday party back in March.'

'It's the dwarf we should be wary of. He's one mean bastard. For that reason, I think we should try and take them by surprise. We should be able to get in round the back easily enough.'

'I'll follow your lead on this one.' Hardwick was speeding, his shoulders hunched as he concentrated on the road. 'If we get the chance, let's take the dwarf on first.' His fists clenched tighter on the wheel. 'Then we can tackle the other two and get Lavelle away. You'd better go up against Braithwaite. If I do it, I'll probably kill him, the way I feel right now.'

★　★　★

'Better pull in here,' suggested Blake. 'Last thing we want is for whoever's inside to hear us approaching.'

They got out of the car and strode determinedly into the grounds, passing the large wrought-iron gate. Tanis Towers was in darkness. Moonlight filtered through the dense, voluminous clouds, throwing grotesque shadows from the crenellated towers across the lawn.

Parked at the end of the drive was Braithwaite's car. 'Well it looks like he's here,' commented Hardwick.

'So it would seem. Come on.' There was, as Blake had anticipated, no real difficulty in getting into the house. Within minutes, he had found a window with a loose catch. It was not difficult to ease it up and force it open. After a brief scramble, both he and Hardwick were inside, moving noiselessly across one of Lavelle's ground-floor rooms.

There was a muffled noise coming from upstairs — a strange, chiming kind of sound intermingled with a shrill whistling that whilst not unpleasant, played havoc with the imagination, conjuring up all sorts of unnatural things.

'What the hell's that?' whispered Hardwick.

Blake shrugged his shoulders and switched on his torch. 'God knows. It sounds almost hypnotic. Better not listen to it too hard. Stay close behind me,' he said softly. 'And whatever you do, don't be too quick with that axe you're carrying. We don't want another murder on our hands if we can help it.' The disturbing, paranoid suspicion that Braithwaite had planted earlier — that the American was the one responsible for the trail of death which he had been following — flashed though his mind. The thought that Hardwick was now behind him with an axe filled him with a dark dread. Was it conceivable that he was being brought here like a lamb to the slaughter? Quickly he dismissed the idea, well aware that thinking along those lines would do no good.

They moved out into a wide corridor, the door to the study facing them. Blake listened, glancing about him suspiciously. At the end of the corridor he could make out the grand entrance hall, the stairs a well of darkness leading to the upper floor. Looking into that blackness, he slipped his hand into his jacket pocket, closing his fingers around the stout handle of his blackjack.

They made their way slowly up the stairs, eyes upward, expectant and alert. But nobody appeared there. At the top they turned right across the landing, into another corridor that was broader than the one downstairs. Tall portraits in gilt frames stared down at them from either side.

Blake's sense of unease grew until it became almost unbearable. Whilst that spine-tingling music drifted out of the shadows he wanted to scream, to send his own voice echoing throughout the upper floor of the house. He shuddered and pulled himself together. Knowing the layout of the place, he was certain that the source of the noise was a large room that Lavelle had obviously used as a more private living room than the one downstairs. The door was slightly ajar. Signalling to Hardwick for silence and putting his torch back in his jacket, he crept forward.

The first thing Blake saw as he peered around the door was a sight not for the fainthearted — Zeb's broad and fleshy buttocks. The dwarf had his back to him and, apart from an obscene codpiece and a mask, he was naked.

The furniture had been pushed to the edges and the room was lit with half a dozen strategically placed old-fashioned oil lamps. Three metal stands were interspersed between the lamps. Resting atop each one was a severed head. Blake immediately recognised Jennings, and the middle head still retained enough of its grisly features for him to know it was Snell. The third, however, had decomposed so much that only scraps of flesh clung to the skull. This had to be Ryan.

In the centre of the room, resting on a trestle table, was the sarcophagus from the study. Leaning over it, dressed in a dark robe and a tall, mitre-like crown, his hands and face blackened with shoe polish to resemble the statuette of the ebon-skinned pharaoh, was Braithwaite. The effect was impressive, although his spectacles were rather incongruous. On his immediate left, wearing strange robes and strumming a peculiar musical instrument resembling a harp, was his wife, Henrietta. A smell of incense filled the room.

There was a surreal quality about what he was seeing that threatened Blake's sanity. It was like something from a Monty Python sketch. He did not know whether to scream or laugh. However, the decision was made for him when Braithwaite reached down into the coffin and removed Lavelle's severed head.

'*You evil bastards!*' snarled Hardwick, who was now in the doorway. In a mad rush he charged Braithwaite, shouldering Zeb aside.

Despite his age, Braithwaite was quick. Pulling a revolver from the pocket of his robe, he fired two shots into the American. Even as Hardwick crumpled to the thick carpet, the horror writer raised the gun and shot off another three bullets at Blake. All three rounds blasted into the thick wood of the door as Blake threw himself back into the corridor, his heart racing.

His tongue lolling from the bizarre face-mask he wore, Zeb sprang from the room and was greeted by a hefty whack to the side of his head from Blake's blackjack. Stumbling to one side, the dwarf grasped at the wall, pulling himself to his feet.

The bangs from the gunshots ringing in his ears, Blake brought the club down again, cracking it over the midget's back. There came another deafening report and he felt a bullet whiz past his head. He then heard a click and a curse and risked a look round the door to see Braithwaite throw the spent gun to one side.

The 'mad pharaoh' reached down and, using both hands, picked up a replica khopesh — a curved, heavy-bladed ancient Egyptian sickle-sword, its length smeared with fresh blood.

Common sense shouted at Blake to run. To flee from this madness whilst he had the chance. When he was safe and far from here he could phone the police. Let them deal with it. However, he knew that if he were to do that then Hardwick would certainly die — assuming of course that he was not already dead.

'Kill him, Charles! Kill the defiler!' Henrietta spat venomously.

Braithwaite looked at her and nodded. 'It will be done, O Daughter of Set!' He advanced, his movements slow, his eyes fixed on the private investigator, boring into him with utter malignity. It was clear that he was struggling with the heavy sword. In unskilled hands it may well have made a fine sacrificial weapon against someone they had probably drugged, but how good it would prove in combat was something else entirely.

Still, it was long and it was sharp and Blake had no desire to be on its receiving end. He pulled back and threw his blackjack at the advancing figure, cursing as it missed.

'You're too late — you cannot kill me! *I*

am *immortal*!' Braithwaite proclaimed triumphantly. 'The ritual is complete! I've crossed the Abyss! My *ka* no longer walks in the Great Shadow!'

'You're not immortal, you're insane!' Blake continued to retreat along the corridor. There must be something he could do. If Braithwaite tried a lunge with the sword, he should be able to dodge it, maybe even wrestle it away from him.

Henrietta emerged from the living room. A second later, she screamed terribly as one of the oil lamps smashed against her. Her robe caught fire and she tried desperately to beat at the flames. Zeb scrambled to his feet and leapt away from her, fearful for his bare skin.

Braithwaite turned and looked in horror at his burning wife.

Seizing his chance, Blake hurled himself forward, arms outstretched. Grabbing Braithwaite round the waist, he threw him to the floor, knocking the khopesh out of his knobbly hands. To his relief, he saw Hardwick stumble through the doorway, holding on to the jamb. In the room Henrietta was still ablaze, her gown almost completely burnt away.

Hardwick slammed the door shut and called to Blake: 'Let's get the hell out of here! There's nothing we can do for Jeremy!' Blood was dripping between the fingers of the hand clamped to his left shoulder.

Blake launched a savage kick into Braithwaite, doubling him up. He then reached for the khopesh.

Zeb got to it first. Hefting the heavy sword in both hands and realising that the man in the doorway was wounded, he concluded that Hardwick posed a lesser threat and made a rush at Blake.

This time Blake's courage faltered and he turned and ran. The dwarf pursued him, jumping over the recumbent Braithwaite.

Heart thumping, Blake sprang down the stairs, looking for some kind of weapon to defend himself with. The only illumination was the moonlight shining through the hall windows. He ran for the front door but found it locked.

Coming down the stairs towards him was the squat, oily figure of Zeb. With a curse, the homicidal dwarf swung the khopesh round in a wide arc. Narrowly dodging it, Blake leaped in, grabbed the midget by the hair and kicked him full in the groin. He then brought the other's head down to meet his rising knee — an attack which sent Zeb reeling into the wall and knocked the weapon from his hands. Striding over, he hauled the dwarf to his feet, tore away his mask and smote a powerful right hook into his jaw, knocking him out cold. Assured that Zeb would be causing no further trouble for a while, he began back up the stairs.

The corridor was empty.

Blake stared in confusion for a moment before noticing that the door which gave access to the roof was ajar. Rushing over, he pushed it wide and climbed the stairs, the cold night air refreshing him. The outer door at the top was wide open. He stepped outside. With a lurch of his heart, he saw that Hardwick had managed to get Braithwaite halfway over the rooftop parapet.

'Neither you nor Jeremy understood what could be achieved. I was the only one who had the courage and vision to do this. You only care about money,' Braithwaite shouted, struggling to be heard over the wind and rain. The boot polish was washing off and running in black rivulets down his face, revealing the pale, wrinkled skin beneath. It looked like he was melting.

'You call this *courage?* Killing people, killing friends?'

'It had to be done. Once I had understood my precious book the path was clear to me. Snell tried to betray me. He stole the book. After I killed him, I ransacked his house but couldn't find it. And then, my prayers to Set were answered . . . Thanks to you and your stupid detective, you delivered it straight into my hands.'

'You stupid, selfish bastard. The old magics don't work like that. None of this would've given you eternal life. You've murdered four men, one of whom treated you with nothing but kindness, and you've achieved nothing!'

'*Nothing?* We'll see about that shall we?' Braithwaite's eyes shone with madness. With a sudden lunge, his claw-like hands grabbed Hardwick and pulled, throwing himself backwards over the parapet. Taken off balance, Hardwick started to flip over. Blake ran forward and was just in time to grab the American by the lower legs as he overbalanced completely.

For a handful of seconds, Braithwaite maintained his grip, dangling over the edge. Then there was a loud rip as Hardwick's coat tore along a seam and Braithwaite was falling into the darkness.

There was a mad laugh and then a moment later a sickening thud.

With an almighty heave, Blake dragged Hardwick back over the parapet and they sat panting on the roof.

★   ★   ★

Blake had given up smoking months ago, but all the same he had readily accepted a cigarette from Hardwick. A bottle of whisky would have been better given the circumstances, but right now anything to soothe his frayed nerves was welcome. The police had arrived a few minutes ago in answer to his call. They had decided to tell the truth about everything. Whether or not they would be believed was something only time would tell. A stern-faced detective had taken a look at Braithwaite's crumpled body and had then started to bombard them with questions, during which time an ambulance arrived.

The ambulance men were directed inside and shortly brought out a stretcher with Henrietta's barely conscious and smouldering form. She was groaning and mumbling to herself. Two policemen escorted Zeb out of the house, a look of utter bewilderment on their faces. Clearly apprehending a half-naked, well-oiled dwarf was far from routine.

Leaving Blake and Hardwick in the company of one of his constables, the detective went over to the ambulance staff. 'One of these men has been shot and you've got a dead one over there.'

'Okay. I'll just check.' One of the ambulance men knelt down beside Braithwaite's body. A few seconds later, he exclaimed: 'There's a pulse!'

Blake and Hardwick looked at each

other in astonishment.

'That's impossible!' Blake said. 'He can't have survived that fall.'

One of the ambulance men examining Hardwick looked over his shoulder at the private investigator. 'People do, sometimes. At that height it's all down to luck. I'd expect him to have some very serious injuries though, both internal and external.'

'I certainly hope so,' growled Hardwick. 'He should've died for what he did.'

'You don't think . . . ' Blake said hesitantly.

'*No, I do not!*' Hardwick snapped. 'It's just coincidence. If he pulls through the only life he'll be enjoying will be a life sentence.'

★　★　★

At six o'clock in the evening of the following day, Blake wearily unlocked the street door leading to his office. The police had kept him and Hardwick at the station overnight and for most of that day. They were not officially under suspicion, but even Hardwick had decided that the only way to avoid being arrested immediately was to do everything asked of them. They had answered hour upon hour of questions, helping the police to understand the breadth of Braithwaite's murderous machinations. Officers had been despatched to the house in Adder Brook and shortly after, Kagga had been brought to the station.

At that point the tension had begun to ease. It seemed that the mad Hungarian had, unusually for him, done some thinking and realised his best bet was to spill everything he knew to the interpreter they had managed to find, safe in the knowledge that he, at least according to *him*, had not killed anyone.

More of the story had come out then — the meetings between Snell and Braithwaite, the decision to 'haunt' Tanis Towers which had been carried out by Zeb and Kagga with Snell's head, and a few tricks they had picked up from an illusionist who used to tour with the circus. Braithwaite had it planned to the minute and was waiting till the specified time to call Lavelle so he could be guaranteed to find the man scared and vulnerable to the offer of sanctuary. The house at Adder Brook was big enough for the two Hungarian oddities to stay there undetected by Lavelle, who was by that point being drugged — firstly to make him hallucinate and then to sedate him for the horrible ritual that ended his life.

Kagga's evidence cleared Blake and Hardwick of any involvement in the murders, although they would still have to explain their actions in not informing the police. Hardwick had promised to hire a good lawyer to represent them but Blake could see his employer was badly shaken by the whole affair. After all, if he *had* gone to the police right at the beginning, Lavelle might not have been killed — although Blake privately doubted it. Someone as insane as Braithwaite would have done his utmost to find another way if the first plan had failed. It chilled his blood to think of the Braithwaites calmly deliberating with Snell how they would kill Ryan, and then turning against Snell too. According to Kagga, Zeb had thrown in his lot with Braithwaite after that and they had been working for the horror writer ever since. If Braithwaite ever regained consciousness, which Blake sincerely hoped he would not, he was definitely destined for Broadmoor.

Eventually they had been allowed to leave, with the usual cautions and the distinct likelihood of a future arrest for obstructing the police. Hardwick had driven them back to his house, where Blake's car was still waiting, the journey almost silent as each thought over the terrible events of the night before.

* * *

Relieved to be home, Blake opened the door to his stairwell. He stopped dead. Something was wrong. Had he seen a flash of light under his office door? Possibilities raced through his head. Had Zeb somehow escaped and come to finish him off? Was Horn or someone else a part of the unholy group? For a moment he imagined Braithwaite himself, miraculously recovered from his injuries and waiting to exact a dreadful revenge. He battled against the urge to flee. If he ran now, he would always live in fear. Better to face whatever it was. Besides, he had the advantage of being on home turf.

Quietly opening the cupboard under the stairs, he removed the baseball bat he kept there. It had three long, sharp nails driven through its head and he felt considerably better with it in his hands. Advancing up the stairs, he booted the door open.

Sitting on a chair, with his feet up on Blake's desk, was the formidable figure of Benny McQuire. One of his skinhead thugs was standing behind him, looking menacingly at Blake.

McQuire removed the cigar from his mouth and fixed the private investigator with a steely stare. 'And where have you been, Mr Blake? Not forgotten my job, have you?'

Blake sighed with unfeigned relief. McQuire and his heavy he could cope with. He set down the bat and pulled the free chair up to the desk, surprising the burly Irishman who had expected quite a different response. 'Benny! Christ, you're a sight for sore eyes, my friend. Sorry I haven't been in touch.' He kicked off his shoes and relaxed into the chair. 'You wouldn't believe the week I've had.'

THE END

We do hope that you have enjoyed reading this large print book.

Did you know that all of our titles are available for purchase?

We publish a wide range of high quality large print books including:
Romances, Mysteries, Classics General Fiction Non Fiction and Westerns

Special interest titles available in large print are:
The Little Oxford Dictionary Music Book, Song Book Hymn Book, Service Book

Also available from us courtesy of Oxford University Press:
Young Readers' Dictionary (large print edition) Young Readers' Thesaurus (large print edition)

For further information or a free brochure, please contact us at:
Ulverscroft Large Print Books Ltd., The Green, Bradgate Road, Anstey, Leicester, LE7 7FU, England. Tel: (00 44) **0116 236 4325 Fax:** (00 44) **0116 234 0205**

Other titles in the
Linford Mystery Library:

MISTER BIG

Gerald Verner

Behind all the large-scale crimes of recent years, the police believe there is an organising genius. The name by which this mysterious personality has become familiar to the press, the police and the underworld is Mister Big. When murder and kidnapping are added to his crimes, Superintendent Budd of Scotland Yard becomes actively involved. Eventually the master detective uncovers a witness who has actually observed and recognised Mister Big leaving the scene of a murder — but before he can tell Budd whom he has seen, he is himself murdered!

FIVE GREEN MEN

V. J. Banis

Nancy's vacation at her aunt's San Francisco mansion takes a nightmarish turn when she is attacked by a mysterious thief of ancient jade figurines. Her assailant's vows to kill her are very nearly successful more than once. Can she trust the stranger who has been following her ever since her arrival in the city, even though his intervention saves her life? Then she must contend with a murder she is powerless to stop, and the return of her father, who she'd been told had died when she was a child . . .

THE SCENT OF HEATHER

V. J. BANIS

Maggie and her sister Rebecca come to Heather House to recover from the drowning deaths of their two husbands. But the house seems to be haunted by the ghost of its one-time owner, Heather Lambert, the scent of the eponymous herb occasionally drifting through the air. As Maggie falls under the spell of the house, events take a more sinister turn when she narrowly survives an attempt on her life, and then the housekeeper is found murdered . . . Can Maggie discover the secret of Heather House before it's too late?